RAW MATERIAL

Sue Wilsea's work is with words, whether that's writing, performing or teaching. Her fiction and poetry has been widely published and broadcast, and 2012 saw the publication of her first collection of short stories, *Staying Afloat*. In 2014 she gained an MA in Creative Writing from Newcastle University. As a freelance Arts practitioner Sue currently delivers Creative Writing classes and undertakes a wide range of writing / literature-based projects. She has four grown-up children, lives with her husband in North Lincolnshire and buys too many books and earrings.

by the same author

STAYING AFLOAT

Raw Material

SUE WILSEA

Valley Press

First published in 2016 by Valley Press
Woodend, The Crescent, Scarborough, YO11 2PW
www.valleypressuk.com

First edition, first printing (October 2016)

ISBN 978-1-908853-78-3
Cat. no. VP0095

Cover and text design by Jamie McGarry

Printed and bound in Great Britain by
Charlesworth Press, Wakefield

Supported using public funding by
ARTS COUNCIL
ENGLAND

LOTTERY FUNDED

Contents

Acknowledgements

'The Big Idea' won second prize at the 2016 Ilkley Literature Festival. 'What's Underneath' and 'A Blue Dress' were first published as a pamphlet by Wombach Press (2015). 'Words, Words, Words' won the Vogel Prize (2013). 'A Bench and a Ladder' was published in *Alliterati* (2014) and 'View from the Top' in *Firewords* (2014). 'Honeypot' appears by kind permission of Moth Publishing: it was published in *Northern Crime 1* (2015). 'Scarborough Warning' first appeared in *Tales from the Yorkshire Coast* (Snow Books 2014).

The Big Idea

ONCE I'VE ZIPPED through my typing, I leaf through my notebook – you know the one that writers are meant to have on them at all times so they can jot down a startling image, snippets of overheard conversation and those germs of ideas that will eventually blossom into a bestselling novel.

There are a lot of lists, all of them with one item not crossed out but transferred to another list. I notice that smoked chilli oil appears on four lists until eventually being struck through with a thick black marker pen, although I don't remember buying any; also lists of recommended books and newspaper articles (a writer needs an enquiring mind); domestic jobs: replace washer in downstairs loo, stain removal, contact Council re new recycling box; long term objectives: re-start fitness regime, register on dating sites. I used to tear out the pages with completed lists but then it looked as if I'd done nothing. Achieved nothing.

It's not all lists. There's a scrabble score from when Matt and Alison came round last week. Alison won, as usual, but only because Matt opened up a triple word for her and he knew she had a Q and a U because I caught him glancing at her tiles while topping up her glass. Basically, they were working as a team – against me – which really pissed me off. I won't have them over again. Actually, I might have told them that. I'd drunk too much and for two turns I'd had nothing but vowels.

But, make no mistake, this is a writer's notebook. I

have a lot of brilliant opening lines. Admittedly, getting beyond the opening lines is more difficult. Sometimes I'll get as far as writing a page or two but I soon lose interest. That's only because I haven't found my Big Idea yet.

When I decide to kidnap Stephen obviously I need a list. There are items to be purchased such as gaffer tape and the necessary drugs; there are things to check out like his routine after work and his living arrangements. Having read a lot of crime novels I appreciate how important it is to cover my tracks so my lists are in code. I also know that I must not rush things. By nature a methodical person, I can tend towards impatience when I'm in the grip of my 'enthusiasms'. I must proceed carefully. But I wasn't careful enough: the stain was a mistake.

Let me tell you about Stephen. I've written him into one of my stories – well, the first bit, it's not finished yet. I describe him as a *'bird of prey, sharp featured with piercing eyes and a shock of black hair.'* A little artistic licence as in fact he's short-sighted and his eyes tend to peer rather than pierce. The dark hair is right, although when I passed his desk the other day I noticed he's starting to go thin on top. If anyone's the bird of prey, of course it's me but there you go, that's the power of fiction!

I like Stephen but I don't think he likes me. I'm not saying he *dis*likes me. Though he might do. I overheard him at the copier, talking about someone to Joyce, saying she was weird and creepy but that could easily apply to my colleagues Jane and Lily. Jane has an eating disorder and is always furtively nibbling at what looks like hamster food which she brings to work in little plastic boxes, each labelled for different times of the day. About half an hour after eating, regular as clockwork, she'll scamper off to the Ladies and puke it all up. She's pretty but thinks she's ugly. Lily is into Steam Punk at weekends and although she tones it down for the office her make-up is crazy – green nails, so much purple blusher she looks as if she's gone ten rounds and racoon eyes. Plus she's fat and bi-sexual. Both of them are rich pickings for characterisation: in fact I plan to give Jane a series of monologues which will reveal that her eating disorder stems from her rape, by a close family member when she was twelve, while Lily will be my main protagonist in a play (working title *Our Times, Your Times*) in which she will go into a time warp, become a zombie and save the world from global warming.

So in all probability it wasn't me Stephen was talking about. After all, I present as very normal. I often laugh to myself when I think of how they will react when my genius is discovered and I am revealed as the writer of award-winning fiction.

Using the term *kidnap* earlier was probably not the best choice. As a wordsmith, I should be more precise. My aim is to entice him back to my place and then … well, I haven't got it figured out to the last detail yet but with all the best stories you never know exactly how they will end. The gaffer tape and drugs were a device to heighten dramatic tension but you have to admit it worked!

Stephen agrees to come round – that morning I arrive at the office before anyone else and leave a note on his desk. He keeps his head down for most of the day but once he's turned off his computer and put on his coat he comes across to my desk and says thanks for the invite to supper the following evening, he'd love to come. Out of the corner of my eye I can see Jane gawping and Lily sniggering. Up yours, I think.

Obviously a list is called for. In fact, I end up writing

loads of them as I keep changing my mind about what to cook and how many cleaning jobs I can get done in the time available. I stay up virtually all night and fill three whole notebooks and I have to admit part of me is thinking why can't I write as much as this when I'm attempting to be creative? In the morning I am so tired that going into work is out of the question. When I ring the office Lily answers so I have to trust her with the truth and ask her to pass on a message to Stephen: he is still to come round this evening. She gives one of her stupid sniggers but agrees to tell him.

What do I want from Stephen? Sex – obviously – but also someone who will take an interest in me as a person, which means me as a writer. Apart from anything else, I'll need someone to manage my career, negotiate film rights and so on, but also someone to accompany me to book signings, manage the crowds, always be there at my side. Stephen seems dependable – he doesn't go out drinking with the other blokes in the office and he works hard – but it's the fact that he's always got his head in a book which convinces me he's the right one.

He arrives and it's awkward but becomes slightly less so after the first bottle of wine. I serve up food – Waitrose ready meals which taste better than anything I could have cooked. I do most of the talking but he seems OK with that. We go upstairs and have sex. Stephen does look better horizontal and without his glasses but despite my best efforts he doesn't stay hard for long. However, that could be nerves and I decide to give him the benefit of the doubt. At any rate, it's all research. That's the great thing about being a writer: however shit an experience is (and believe me I'm in the Premier League of Those Who Have Had Shit Experiences) it's all material you can use at some point. Afterwards, when we're sitting up in bed I read him the synopsis for my latest novel idea. I'm very excited because I think it's possible that this is The Big One – the idea that will create my literary reputation, not to mention make me a lot of money. Obviously I don't want to give too much away (there's no copyright on ideas!) but suffice it to say, it includes someone who lives the same life over and over again, an Alzheimer's patient and a man on a bus who's witness to a murder.

When I finish reading, and once I hear it aloud I have to admit it probably does need a bit of fine tuning, he laughs, the first time I've seen him completely let go (and that includes our recent action between the sheets). It's not a nice gentle laugh but one where he throws his head back and gives a massive guffaw and I can see all his fillings. When he manages to get himself under control he asks if he can see it and reluctantly I hand over the piece of paper. Then he's off again, shaking with laughter so much that the bed is jiggling and that makes me mad. Really mad. Things go fluttery. I reach down into my sewing basket which I keep at the side of the bed, take out my shears and with one thrust stab them into his neck. There's the briefest of moments when our eyes lock and he looks surprised. Then there's lots of spurting blood and within seconds I'm covered with splatters as is the wall behind the headboard which starts to look like a modern abstract painting. Meanwhile, Stephen is making strange gurgly noises and his eyes are rolling around like marbles. The shears are still stuck in so I give a good hard tug and pull them out. It's like I've unplugged a dam: the blood pours out and puddles of it lie in the creases of the sheets. I can see that no amount of soaking is ever going to make the bedding usable again which is annoying to say the least. Once again by having abandoned planning and acting on impulse all I've done is make life more difficult for myself. I should mention the smell too (an important tip for writers is to make sure you appeal to all the senses). As you'd expect, it's iron like, quite intense and heady but in the interests of authenticity I have to add that there's also a strong reek of faeces. I'm not going to look but I assume Stephen has shat himself.

There's no denying I now have a massive problem, namely a body, disposal thereof. I go downstairs, neck the rest of the wine and make a list. It is not a long one:

1.   Bury him.
2.   Incinerate him.
3.   Dump him at sea.

1 requires a spade, 3 requires a boat and both require physical strength. I have none of these things. Number 2 is an easy winner. Somehow I will get Stephen into his car and then drive it to a place where I can torch it, thereby destroying any forensic evidence. Admittedly it's not common for cars to be torched on this estate but I will ensure, through subtle hints, that the police think Stephen got himself involved in a drugs ring or extortion racket and has been hunted down by the gang he's double-crossed. His bookish manner will prove to be an excellent cover (no pun intended) for his criminal life-style. Now my mind is fizzing. My heart pounds and my fingertips tingle as blood races to every nerve end. I am on fire with ideas – I am writing the story!

As far as the police are concerned I won't deny Stephen was in my house. In fact, I will admit we had sex but I'll say that he left about midnight, fifteen minutes from now. Just as they are finishing the interview I'll add, very casually not so it seems like a big deal, that he did seem on edge and that he'd peered out of the window several times during the evening as if he was worried he was being watched.

Practicalities. What I will do is roll him in the duvet, like a Swiss roll, then push him down the stairs. His car is in the carport which adjoins the kitchen so I can take him out that way. Once he's safely stowed on the back seat I will drive to the other side of the estate, near the woods. I should add that I will be dressed in his clothing and will give a toot on the horn as I leave just in case any of my nosy neighbours are watching. Once I've set the car on fire, it shouldn't be long before the petrol tank explodes. Obviously I'll wear gloves, even petty thieves know to do this nowadays, but not everyone is clever enough to cover their feet with Lidl plastic carrier bags which is what I will do. Once the deed is done I will disappear into the woods, emerging onto the B2743. Just a short walk along this quiet road and then I can enter my house through the back gate. This should give me at least half an hour to clean up.

Just as I'm ready to unleash Plan A, a Plan B catches me unawares. This is the problem when one's creative powers are so great and the skill lies in not rejecting a Plan B just because you've invested so much time and emotional energy into your Plan A. Whichever works the best (and sometimes there will be plans C, D, E and F) needs to be the one you pick. I have to conclude that Plan B is simpler and less risky. It is this: Stephen tried to rape me and I fought him off with the nearest thing to hand. I have been in a state of shock for the last half an hour or so hence the delay in calling the police. This makes much more sense. There were weaknesses in Plan A. Forensics would have been able to discover that it was my duvet in the car – how could I have overlooked that?

I dial 999 but it's nearly an hour before they arrive which is pretty shocking but I'd told them he was dead and that I'd done it so I suppose they reckoned there was no urgency. I was disappointed that there were no blue lights or siren though. Anyway, when at last a patrol car draws up outside I have the front door open before the two officers are even halfway up the path.

'Now then, Rosa,' says the older one, 'What's up?'

'I said on the phone. I've killed him. But he was trying to … to…' I start crying and shuddering and find I can't stop. All that adrenaline from before has leaked out and I feel like an empty husk (even *in extremis* I am able to note that this is an impressively vivid image).

Both officers are in the hall and the younger one looks embarrassed. Perhaps it's his first body.

'Where is he then?' he asks and through my tears I catch the glimmer of a smile cross his smug face.

'Upstairs, officer,' I say 'In my bedroom, first on the left.'

The older one sighs and indicates that Smug Face should stay where he is. Then he makes his way slowly up the stairs. I assume he will have seen lots of corpses in the course of his career but I still wonder if he will react in some way when he sees Stephen's blood-splattered body. It's a small house and we would easily hear a loud gasp of shock. Maybe he will simply radio for back-up.

He comes back down a few minutes later, his expression blank. 'Inscrutable' is better. A more literary adjective.

'There's no one there, Rosa,' he says, 'Just like the last time. Are you taking the correct amount of medication? We had a call from a Mr Stephen Woodhall earlier this evening to say he was concerned about your state of mind.'

'My state of mind? What's the scumbag been saying?'

Smug Face wasn't even attempting to hide his expression now: he was grinning. 'Mr Woodhall said that after he rejected your … your advances you went a bit crazy.' Slowly and deliberately he took out his notebook and thumbed through a few pages, 'A *nutjob* was the term I believe he used.'

'Alright lad, that's enough,' said Old Kind One sharply. 'Now then, Rosa, first thing in the morning someone is going to contact your Support Worker and get them to come round. Meanwhile, it's late so how about you get yourself off to bed, maybe make yourself a cup of tea first. In fact, PC Williams here will go and put the kettle on, won't you Williams?'

'Yes sir.'

'Does that sound like a good plan, Rosa?'

I nodded. I've learnt from experience that any words that come out of my mouth won't do any good. That's the reason I love my writing so much. Nobody can argue with fiction.

They leave shortly afterwards and I pour the cup of tea Smug Face made me down the sink. Then I go upstairs but with no intention of sleeping. I have another idea and I am absolutely 110% sure this could be the Big One. Going into the bedroom, I crouch down, reach under my bed for the sewing basket and pull it out. My shears are lying on top. It's been a while since I've used them, I realise that now, but I'm not surprised to see that the blades are encrusted with browny-red flakes. I sit on the floor and start to pick them off one by one.

Raw Material

I'M NOT PROUD of where I came from though strangely I remember it with affection. The heat and the stench were really bad but the worst thing had to be the lack of light. Not that the place was in complete darkness. The filthy basement windows did allow for some murky half-light but not enough to stop the little ones having to hold the material right up under their noses when sewing by hand. Often they paused to rub their eyes, as if by so doing they could make themselves see better. When machining their small heads were bowed so they looked as if they were praying. And after they'd done their twelve hours and emerged into the daylight they blinked just like the plump rats that sauntered through the slum alleyways.

It was Shilpa who cut and stitched me and it felt good. I loved the sensation of her scissors shearing through the rough chalk lines, her needle jab jab jabbing in and out, my seams emerging from under the claw of the machine that she guided. That might seem weird but I always thought it must be like the agony of birth because once I had my shape – a back and a front, two short sleeves and a neck-hole – that's the point I came into being and all the pain was forgotten. It was good being trimmed too, feeling my unwanted bits fall onto the ground. In time they would be swept up and I had fun imagining my remnants as part of another creation. A label was sewn into the back of my neck. This said *Made in India,* which was true, and *Fairtrade* which was not true.

The big question was always whether you'd have something printed on your front or back, or both. I ended up with words only on the front but that didn't matter: the lettering was bright pink, each stroke or curve a thick line which bled into the black cotton. The message was heat sealed on and that was enjoyable, too, being branded, feeling the material warming and the fibres sealing the print. It hurt, of course it did, but what was the alternative? To have no identity, to be a nothing, a no-one. Then there was some glue banged on and glitter. It wasn't done carefully – nothing was – and some of my lettering stayed unembellished while glitter shimmered to the floor and lay there mixed with the sawdust.

Of course the journey was long and dark and being packed so tightly against others was hard. More of my glitter came off and I felt chafed by the unevenness of my seams. It was degrading really. They could have been taking us anywhere and we all knew that wherever it was we'd be sold cheap. Some always liked to make out that we were going to a better life where we'd be worn with pride and treated with respect but I think that deep down everyone knew the truth. And what was that truth? Simply that never again would we experience the love and care we'd had in the sweatshop. Once, when Adesh the supervisor was driving everyone hard to finish an order, Shilpa went too fast and pricked herself. A bead of blood bulbed then dripped onto my sleeve. Bringing me to her lips she licked it off and then, pressing a tiny bit of discarded material to the spot, absorbed any remaining moisture. I was kissed and healed.

Tracey's breasts press against me, making my lettering stretch over them like two small hillocks. I can feel the stub of her nipples, too. She is hot and under her arms I'm damp. She smells of all the things she puts on her skin: vanilla, honey and almonds. And alcohol of course. I remember the alcohol from when Adesh used to come round and breathe down the necks of the girls while one doughy hand reached down and squeezed between their legs. She spills some of the alcohol over me – the alcohol is disguised with something sweet and fruity.

'Read what it says!' she shrieks at her friend Mandy and I feel ashamed. She pulls me tightly over her breasts, 'Go on! Read it!'

'SEX INSTRUCTOR – FIRST LESSON FREE' she bawls out before Mandy can make any response. Mandy cackles though she can barely stand up. Now she's being sick and a bit splashes onto me. It's yellow, smells like curry and for a brief moment I'm there in the backstreets of Bangalore.

'For fuck's sake Mandy! Now look what you've done – spoilt me new T-shirt, haven't you?'

Mandy is lying in the gutter and you can see up her skirt to a pink cleft and a tuft of straw coloured hair. Some young men, who are also very drunk, are standing on the other side of the road pointing and jeering. I'm put straight into the laundry basket when we get back and that's not nice – on top of me there's her underpants which she stuffed into her pocket before she had sex with one of the young men who'd been laughing. The next day I was washed by Tracey's mother and I got smaller because the water was too hot. In fact, it burned me and feeling my fibres shrinking must be what it's like when the muscles around the heart contract. You could tell Tracey's mother was mad at her and I wasn't at all surprised when, later that day, I ended up in a big bag along with some old toys and a pair of curtains. We all knew about charity shops, of course. A jungle of old clothes jostling for position on overcrowded rails, picked over by people who were poor – at least by the standards of this new land. Again the smell of sweat, there's always sweat, this time not young and fresh but stale, old and stinking of desperation. Of course, that was assuming you made it onto the rails. If you were deemed to be unsaleable even here, that was a death sentence. Textile recycling is a quiet, worthy sounding term and goes nowhere near describing the horror and carnage of the shredder at the mill.

I wasn't chosen to be put on the rails. As old gnarled fingers inspected me I feared the worst but I was spared. Once again I was put in a bag – like me some were shrunk, others were stretched or baggy and all of us were undoubtedly past our best – but my companions were decent sorts and it became obvious that our destination was not the mill. We could sense the silent screams of garments who had been chosen for that fate; some were ripped apart even before they made their final journey and although that was hard to bear we were glad we were the lucky ones.

Another long airless journey, tightly packed together, and when we eventually emerged into the light we discovered ourselves to be in a land not very different from that of our birth. Dark skins, scorching heat, pungent smells of spices, goats, petrol, shit. It was different, though. The skins were more ebony than coffee coloured and it was quieter, especially when we were taken out of the city into the jungle. There was a school there which was run by the same organisation that owned the charity shop. Lots of children were running round but they were bright-eyed and curious, not like the children who made me and my friends. Their little black hands rifled through the large plastic sacks and one after another would screech as they found what they were looking for. Badru chose me. Most of my glitter was gone by now and my lettering was faded so that it more like a smudge on my front but he pulled me on and I could tell by the way he strutted round how pleased he was. They were all dressed in a mismatch of clothes that came from the bags so that they looked like a load of characters from different books written at different times.

It didn't take me long to work out that Badru was smart. He sat on the floor of the wooden hut they called a school and, arms folded tightly across his chest, leaned forward to hear every word the teacher was saying. For the rest of the day he'd repeat his lessons to himself which meant he often got teased by his friends. But he shrugged them off, joined in a game of football from time to time so as to make sure he wasn't left out of their circle, and went on learning. His English steadily improved. Then came the day when he picked me up from the floor of his hut where he slept with his parents and four younger brothers and sisters and, once outside, stopped to trace with his finger the outline of the words that were still just visible on my front. That's when he blushed with shame, scrunched me into a bundle and threw me down onto the dusty ground. Then he stamped on me and each time his foot came down I was aware of its pink underside, like undercooked lamb, and the layers of hardened, calloused skin on his heel. It was like being branded all over again.

Of course Badru didn't want to wear me anymore. Other youngsters used me from time to time but I was soon discarded when fresh supplies arrived in the village. Anyway, Badru was big now. He earned himself money by helping the white American teacher in the school and gradually he began to look more like him, wearing floppy combat cut-offs and red and yellow T-shirts imprinted with the names of baseball teams. In the evening, round the fire, he wore Levi 501s and a hooded sweatshirt with a zip up the front, clothes which arrived in brown paper parcels delivered to him personally.

I have started to wear thin. My fibres were never strong and now don't mesh together as they should. I am frayed around the neckline, my bottom edge droops and what has been solid black is now more like grey with small lighter grey patches, like thumbprints, where the pink lettering once was. Today I am lying in the blazing sun in a sorry pile of other discarded cloth, twisted metal and broken pottery. I feel myself crisping, my threads tightening and becoming brittle, and I wonder how and when the final end will come. The day lengthens. In the jungle, kept at bay by a stockade of posts hammered into a circle, trees are being hacked down. I hear their screams as sap, their lifeblood, trickles slowly and stickily down their trunks. Now I can hear more screams but these are from another distant time. I see row after row of stooped figures, black fingers plucking at clumps of white cotton, while to one side a man or woman, I cannot tell which and anyway it doesn't matter, is being repeatedly struck with a whip. This person is wearing what was a shirt but is now rags and as the whip comes down the shreds of material flutter like streamers.

All of us are continually made and remade and there is comfort in that. All of their hands are on me – Shilpa, Tracey, Badru, even Adesh.

Once I heard one of the ministers say *Out of the darkness and into the light.*

Time shrinks to a ball of spun threads. It whirls.

What's Underneath

MARIE AND SHEILA lightly embrace, lips brushing dry cheeks. Like ash, thinks Marie.

Sheila holds up a bra in mauve gingham trimmed with tiny green bows, 'What do you think?'

'Pretty, very pretty.'

Once Sheila was pretty. Now her hair, unlike her waist, is thinning and her colour is high. She still dresses well though. Black suits her. Marie is aware of her old Parka, scuffed boots and imagines that Sheila's penetrating look has somehow revealed her slack, faded underwear.

'Decided to treat yourself?'

Sheila thrusts the bra back into a thicket of hangers, 'Just browsing really. Don't think I'll bother. How about you? What are you after?'

Marie has no idea. She has not consciously made her way to Debenhams' lingerie department. Or even Debenhams come to that. But the days are long and in department stores you don't need to be focussed. You can drift. Yesterday she spent most of the afternoon in the Men's department choosing outfits for him.

'Marie?'

'Sorry?'

'I asked what...?'

'Oh yes, I'm just browsing too.'

Sheila presses her lips together tightly. A threadworm of lipstick has bled into the corner of her mouth.

'I do need some pyjamas!' In desperation Marie looks around but cannot see nightwear. Maybe it's in a different section. She gets so cold at night. So very cold.

'Marie,' Sheila fiddles with her wedding ring, 'I know this is a dreadful word but how are you…' She inscribes imaginary quotation marks in the air, '…coping?'

Marie doesn't really understand that word but she has a stock response, 'It's difficult but I take it one day at a time … work have been very good and told me to take as much leave as I want. You know, compassionate leave.'

'Compassion!' Sheila snorts, 'You're a fine one to talk about compassion!' She turns away to feign interest in a rack of knickers, raking through the display and knocking a pair to the floor.

None of those would go near you, Marie thinks, and she surprises herself with this petty vindictiveness.

Sheila stoops to pick the knickers up and struggles to put them back in the right place. Her voice is muffled, 'Twenty-six years we were married.'

'I know.' And I only had two, thinks Marie. A sliver from both our lives.

'Anyway, the funeral was lovely. That's probably not the right word but you know what I mean. It did Jonathan proud.'

'Thank you.' Marie knows that it wasn't meant as a compliment and sees that Sheila is on the verge of reacting but instead she moves towards another display. Marie trails after her. She scrabbles after any mention of Jonny's name like a starved animal in search of food. She has made unnecessary calls to the dentist, optician, golf club in order just to be able to say his name.

Sheila has a salmon pink camisole between her thumb and forefinger, rubbing the satin material gently. It slithers and shimmers, 'Sophie read beautifully, didn't she?'

Marie nods, 'Beautifully.'

'And the vicar's address was spot-on. Especially considering the fact that I don't suppose Jonathan had set foot in a church since our wedding.' She let go of the camisole. 'Are you alright, Marie? You look very pale.'

'I might go and get a cup of tea. Would you like…'

'Very kind but I'm in a bit of a rush,' Sheila says, not moving.

Marie hoists her bag onto her shoulder, 'Give Sophie my love and Ben of course. They're very welcome to come over to the flat any time. I haven't seen them since the funeral.'

'I'll certainly pass that on but you know how busy they both are. Naturally they were devastated by their father's death but life has to go on, especially when you're young.' There's only the slightest emphasis on the last word.

Marie's head is light, it's floating away and she's interested to observe the person, apparently her, who suddenly points to a plastic dummy on a display stand at the end of the aisle. The bald dummy has truncated arms which stick out at sharp angles and a blank face which has been given an eye-patch. It is wearing a red and black basque, cinched in at the waist and trailing black suspenders like limpid exclamation marks, unapologetically sleazy, 'How about that?'

Sheila cocks her head to one side, 'Not my style, I'm afraid, though I understand that Jonathan had rather a penchant for the tarty look.'

'I was his partner!' Marie hadn't intended her voice to be so loud. A middle aged woman and her daughter immersed in a close examination of Support Garments in the next aisle bob their heads up expectantly like ducks from under water. Deeply embarrassed Marie sinks to the floor. She sits there hugging her knees to her chest and studying Sheila's black patent court shoes.

Sheila's voice comes from on high, 'I'm fully aware of that, Marie.'

'So why do you have to keep making out that I was some kind of bit on the side!'

'I don't think I've ever suggested anything of the kind. Or at least I didn't mean to…' Sheila's shoulders suddenly slump and she looks round as if she has got off a plane to find herself on the wrong continent, 'To tell you the truth, Marie, I'm not sure what I'm doing at the moment.'

A ping and the tannoy crackles into life with an offer of Double Points on all beauty products. Marie scrambles to her feet and when Sheila remains staring into the distance Marie taps her lightly on the arm.

'Sheila, do you reckon right now Jonny's looking down on the two of us and having a laugh?'

It works. Sheila straightens her back and speaks briskly, 'If that's a serious question, no, because I don't believe in an afterlife. He's gone. The bastard. The fucking bastard.'

Marie smiles, 'He certainly could be.'

'But I loved him.'

'I know. We both did. Do.'

'All this lovely beautiful stuff…' Sheila indicates the ocean of underwear, 'and for most of the time it's hidden. Unseen. Under the surface. It makes no sense.'

'I'm going to get going.'

'How about that cup of tea?'

For so long Sheila has been obsessively curious about this woman who stole her husband. When Jonny first left her she quizzed the children endlessly but they batted away her questions like tiresome flies and, aware that she ran the risk of losing them too, she forced herself to stop asking what Marie looked like, how she behaved, what food she liked, what music she listened to. Marie will never know how many times she, Sheila, followed her home from work and stood on the other side of the road to her block of flats waiting for the light to come on, seeing if she could make out anything before the curtains were closed. In her fantasies Jonathan realised what a huge mistake he'd made and she and Marie had a dramatic showdown. True, these imagined scenarios took place in appropriately spectacular settings – a windswept landscape, a cliff top at sunset or a deserted church – rather than an overheated department store but at least now she has the chance to satisfy her hunger to find out everything she can about Marie. To be able to work out why and how everything turned out as it did.

There is a pause.

'Let's make it another time,' Marie says and they both instinctively know this will never happen. 'Goodbye Sheila and all the very best.'

She turns and pushes through the white-tipped racks which ripple in her wake, leaving the older woman marooned.

The Stories We Tell

PEOPLE ALWAYS USED to put on a sad face when I told them how young I was when Mom died. Not that I ever went out of my way to talk about it and chase the sympathy vote. 'Poor little orphaned me' kind of thing. Anyhow, maybe I wasn't an orphan. My Dad left before I was born so he could have still been out there somewhere. I didn't know and I sure as hell didn't care.

From about the age of three I was brought up by Gran and Gramps and a good upbringing it was too. I remember my childhood fondly: the mountain cabin we stayed in every August; fishing for trout with Gramps; Gran and me making a stack of pancakes; the three of us swimming in the lake by moonlight; back home them cheering me on at the running track; birthdays; Christmas; classmates round for a sleepover; cookouts. There was nothing I missed out on. Mom had me when she was nineteen so Gran and Gramps weren't really old like some of my friends' grandparents. Gramps still went out jogging and Gran enjoyed long, boozy lunches with her female pals. Both of them liked movies and arguing about politics. (Gran loved Obama whereas Gramps thought he was a disappointment.) They were active members of Amnesty International. Went bowling and ice skating. Invited other couples round for dinner, after which they played loud rock music and did embarrassing dancing. But they never pretended they were anything other than grandparents, even though people sometimes assumed they were my parents. Gently and politely they would be put right, 'No, Alan is our grandson...'

Of course there were problems when I hit puberty – I smoked a bit of weed, got myself a police caution and bombed out a couple of courses – but nothing more than a lot of kids my age were doing and it all righted itself in time. Gran and Gramps were tolerant – some might say too much so – and were always there for me. The first time I came home wasted it was Gramps who held my head over the john while I puked before putting me to bed in the recovery position; in the same way when I got dumped by my first serious girlfriend, Gran didn't ask about it but just patted me on the shoulder and that night brought a tray up to my room with my favourite chicken casserole, something only usually allowed when I was officially ill.

Mom died out west, in California. She'd dropped out of college once she was pregnant, even though Gran and Gramps offered to look after me so that she could continue. Once I was about six months old she packed her bags and announced that she was going to be an actress. There's a photo of me and her the day she left. I'm peering out from one of those papoose things and look grouchy like all babies do. She's got a massive backpack at her feet and another couple of bags slung from one shoulder and she's grinning at the camera and giving a thumbs up. She was lovely – there's no getting away from it: tall, slim, high cheekbones and a mass of tumbling dark brown hair: the sort of person you know you'd have a good time with, someone who would piss you off big time along the way but who would always stick by you when the chips were down.

She never did get to be an actress, well not a proper one. Gran said she got a walk on part in a couple of cat food commercials but mostly she worked in bars and clubs at night while neighbours and friends babysat me. Gran was always at pains to tell me what a good Mom she was, how she spent all her days with me and how she'd take me to playgroup and the park and all that. The thing is, not only did I have no memories of that time, being so young, but because California was a place I'd only seen in the movies and on the TV, it's like my Mom was a fictional character. When Gran told me stories about her, that's what they were – stories – nothing really to do with me and my life. When she died Gran and Gramps flew out and brought me back with them after the funeral. The first thing I really remember was playing in the backyard on a rocking horse that Gramps made for me. It seemed massive but I guess that was because I was so young. The horse had everything: a saddle, stirrups, reins and a tail made out of really coarse stuff that I liked pulling out and tickling the inside of my nostrils with.

One thing was for sure, I didn't inherit my Mom's adventurousness. I travelled to a lot of different lands but only in my imagination while on that rocking horse. After graduation, I worked at the local bank in our small mid-western town and that was good enough for me. I was given the nod I'd be Assistant Manager before long and me and Louise, my fiancée, were busy saving up for our wedding. I had my own apartment. Much though I loved Gran and Gramps, it never occurred to me not to move out once I'd got myself a regular job and, though they'd never admit it in a million years, they must have been glad to see me leave too. They liked Louise and we went over most Sundays for brunch after which the women talked wedding dresses and guest lists and Gramps and I watched the ball game. Regular stuff which suited me just fine.

'Doesn't it bother you, marrying Mr Ordinary?' I would say to Louise in a joking way and her response was always the same, reassuring yet weirdly frustrating.

'Ordinary's just fine with me.'

The day it happened, a Thursday, started as usual. It had been a good week. I'd met all my targets easily and that night Louise and I were going out to dinner – not a usual night for us to do so but it was a kind of anniversary: three years since our first date. At lunchtime my colleagues were celebrating the fortieth birthday of one of the cashiers. People had brought in cake and cookies and helium filled balloons, buffeted by the air con, bobbed around her desk. I was pretty sure that some of the staff had more than apple juice in their paper cups but I wasn't planning on saying anything. My reputation, I knew, was of someone a bit straight-laced, someone who always played by the rules but for some reason that day there was an unfamiliar recklessness fizzing round the edges of my consciousness.

I do remember staring at the birthday banner which had been pinned diagonally across the notice board and thinking how old forty was and wondering what Louise and me would be doing at that age. By then we'd have a couple of kids and a decent sized house, I reckoned. Possibly a motor home too. If I made manager, which I should do, we could have family holidays abroad, maybe even explore Europe.

'Someone is asking for you at the front desk, Alan!' called Gretchen from the doorway. She was our main receptionist: statuesque, Nordic, she wore her beauty carelessly like an old coat. She must have been able to have her pick of men but as far as I knew she was unattached. Rumour had it that she was a lesbian but I'd always assumed that was a way of explaining her singledom rather than having any factual basis. I sometimes fantasised about hurting her. I raised my arm in acknowledgement, not sorry to have an excuse to leave the crowded open plan office area, and made my way to the foyer. Seated on one of the orange moulded plastic chairs was a petite brunette. Jabbing at a cell phone, her forehead was ridged with concentration. Gretchen was back behind the reception desk in front of her computer. Without looking up from the screen she said, 'Marian Litten from *New People* magazine.'

'Thanks,' I said awkwardly, feeling my cheeks warm. Gretchen always made me feel like a horny teenager. I approached Ms Litten, clearing my throat as I did so but if she was aware of my presence she gave no indication.

I produced an artificial cough, 'Alan Brelling. Senior Accounts Manager. How can I help you?'

She looked up then and smiled though the smile did not reach her eyes which remained flinty. Deftly slipping the cell into her shoulder bag she stood, offering me her hand.

'Just a few minutes of your time please Mr Brelling.'

Did I know then that those few minutes would invert my reality? No, of course I didn't. But without doubt I was slightly uneasy. It wasn't just the cool clothes, the designer bag or the stylish asymmetrical cut of her hair: Ms Litten brought with her the reek of the big city and the air was tight with it. My palms were damp as I led her into one of our interview rooms. We faced each other across the small conference table, somehow, without me registering the movement, she'd produced a spiral notepad and a pen from her bag. In this particular show, she was the magician and I was the stooge.

'It's about Veronica,' I must have looked blank because she added, 'Your mother.'

'My mother? Ronni. She was always called Ronni.' Then it clicked how bizarre this was, 'She's been dead for over twenty-five years! What do you...'

'I'm sorry to have caught you unawares, Mr Brelling or may I call you Alan? I'm a feature writer for *New People* magazine and we're planning a series of articles on children who have successfully managed to escape a past trauma.'

'I'm sorry but I have no idea what you're talking about,' Anger was rapidly replacing bewilderment, 'As you are aware, this is my workplace and not somewhere to discuss personal matters. Although, having said that, I'm afraid I'm not willing to discuss any aspect of my personal life with you.' I scraped back my chair and stood over her but she remained seated, 'So unless there's something related to your banking affairs with which I can be of assistance then I...'

'I presume you know how your mother died?'

'In an accident. Good day.' I had my back to her with my hand on the door handle when she then spoke those three words that filled up the space in my head and, as seconds passed, expanded into every fibre of my being. So tightly had I gripped the handle that later I found its perfect imprint on the soft cushion of flesh near my thumb.

Ten minutes later I walked out of the bank, never to return. I was nearly knocked down by a car on Eastern Avenue and for many months afterwards I wished only that my body had impacted with hot hard steel and that I had been flung onto the sidewalk to die. I would have wanted my limbs to be grotesquely contorted, my guts to be a pulpy mess, to be shovelled up into a bag like an animal and thrown onto a garbage heap.

Of course those who claimed to love me – Gran, Gramps and Louise – gave every appearance of continuing to do so but I did not want their affection, or rather pity. If I had been a nobler, stronger person perhaps I would have left town like Ronni did. But I didn't. I saw a therapist and in due course Gran, Gramps and I underwent a course of family counselling. As for Louise, she stuck around but I sometimes caught her giving me funny kind of looks, as if she was trying to place this person she once knew a long time ago. We postponed the wedding.

I'd always assumed my grandparents' refusal to let me have toy guns as a child was on account of a shared liberal conscience. Now I knew the real reason: I'd killed their only daughter. Of course everyone constantly asserted my blamelessness:

You were only a toddler…
There's no way you can hold yourself responsible!
It's this country's gun laws that caused the tragedy.

But their words were like those sprinklers they have going all the time in the park in the summer. If it's been too dry and the earth is parched, the grass brown, the water pools, then eventually soaks away making no difference at all.

So many practical aspects fascinated me. How could a toddler have pulled a trigger? Wouldn't the gun have had a safety catch on? Was there a split second when she knew what was going to happen? Where was she hit?

Did I blow her face off? Then more fucking stupid questions would roll around in my skull: what aisle was she in? What was she buying when my chubby little hands reached inside her bag? Was the trolley nearly full or had she just started shopping? Maybe she was distracted by a good-looking guy whose trolley she'd nudged or maybe she was focussed on finding a bargain.

Before that Thursday I thought I had the answers. I don't mean to the big questions – I was no intellectual and never bothered with philosophy – but just how to get myself through the days, weeks, months, years. I'd written my story and the narrative ran like this: if you didn't aspire to be anything other than one of the crowd, if you weren't greedy, worked hard, didn't draw attention to yourself and took care not to over-think life then you managed OK. People who questioned everything were, I'd discovered, generally unhappy. Now my head exploded with questions and not just about the incident itself but about the false construction that was me. If my beginning was not what I'd been led to believe, then how could I be so fucking arrogant and assume I could plan my future.

Was that rocking horse really my first memory? Surely that other memory is there, buried deep in the grey spongy stuff, even if I wasn't able to retrieve it. The flash as the gun fired, the recoil that must have sent me falling from my seat on the supermarket trolley; the fluorescent lights; screaming; alarms; running feet; blood spatters on the floor, the shelves, the display boards; Mom's gasps and gurgles as life drained from her; the sharp tang of ammonia and iron, urine and blood.

New People never used my story. Apart from the fact that I was in no state to play ball with Ms Litten, Gramps threatened to sue her publisher if it ever appeared in print. *YOU SHOT HER*. Like me, Ms Litten blasted a life apart.

I have a gun now and what keeps me awake at night is the thought of squeezing the trigger. Then squeezing it again and again. After all, I've done it once before and that killed the one person I should have loved more than anyone in the world.

So I can't see a problem with strangers.

A Matter of Life and Death

T HERE ARE MANY different ways of dying and at the moment she is experiencing the worst of them. Living. Eva, who never refers to let alone touches her private parts, has recently experienced a large rubber tube up her bottom and a thin plastic one inserted into her bladder. A needle is taped to her left arm and there is a clip on her index finger; two adhesive discs, linked by wires to a monitor, are attached to her chest and an oxygen mask covers nose and mouth. Last night she heard the duty Sister talking on the phone outside her room, saying that Mrs Dawson was 'comfortable'. It took her a while to work out that Sister was talking about her.

In the morning she thinks she has actually died and gone to Heaven. She opens her eyes and sunlight streams through the window onto the bed, drenching the cellular blanket so that it becomes a rich, yellow honeycomb. She feels a new lightness. Lifting one arm in front of her and squinting, she observes its smooth whiteness and the miraculous disappearance of sagging skin flecked with burnished almonds. She'd held her hand out to Richard when he first asked her to dance, a gracious gesture, that of a lady.

She was wearing her black silk gloves, the ones that came up to her elbow and were buttoned with tiny slivers of jet, the ones that her mother said make her look 'common' and 'fast' so she was careful to appear condescending to his invitation. He too had been careful, his hand resting oh so very gently on her waist as he guided her from her seat and through the clutter of tables. Then the band struck up and they were off, gliding, weaving, sweeping around the dance floor, the music in her ears, the soft brush of material against her calves, his leg occasionally touching hers, the smell of shaving soap against her nostrils, an ecstasy of sensual movement.

Now, ready to dance again, she listens for the music but hears only machines. Letting her arm fall down onto the bed the drip tube shudders and the needle settles back into its cushion of purple bruising.

Eva Dawson is 85 and has been very poorly since her operation. Her breathing and heart are being monitored and she's on a drip for nourishment. After the blood transfusion, her white cell count has much improved although she's still having problems breathing independently. She was given an enema this morning to try and deal with some impacted faeces; fluid intake and output are being monitored. Hourly observations needed. Any questions?

Are we turning her, Sister?

Every two hours. She's got a nasty crack on the right buttock that could suppurate if we're not careful and elbows and heels need creaming. Could you draw the curtain, nurse? It's far too bright in here.

Darkness. Shadows. Not yet.

Try as she may, she can't remember the name of the tune the band was playing when Richard asked her to dance for the first time and that at first irritates and then fills her with a desperate sadness. How could she possibly forget something like that? Their tune. What else has she forgotten? She turns her head from side to side in an attempt to shake out the memories.

Eva? Eva, love? Don't go getting yourself all agitated. I'm just going to give you a little prick in the arm to calm you down. There you go.

Richard insisted that their deaths were prepared for thoroughly and sensibly. They made wills, he making provision for her and both of them doing the same for the children. A separate account had been opened for funeral expenses and when he died (quickly and efficiently) she, as instructed, spent exactly half on his funeral. The hymns – 'The Lord's My Shepherd', 'Oh God, Our Help in Ages Past' and 'Guide Me Oh Thou Great Redeemer' – were already chosen, the vicar's speech followed given guidelines by being laudatory but not fulsome and as requested the grandchildren attended on the condition that they sat still without fidgeting in church. No flowers but donations to The Army Benevolent Fund, beer but no spirits at the tea afterwards, medals to the Imperial War Museum and his clothes to any local charity shop except Oxfam.

It was typical, Eva thinks, that she should make a long, messy, drawn out business of dying. Always, it seems, her body has set out to spite her. When, as a young woman, she first bled it was copious and she was forced to lie in bed swaddled between the legs with rags for a whole week while her stomach muscles clenched and twisted with cramps. After it was finished, she assumed that was it. With tightly pressed lips her mother bundled away both the rags and any hope of discussion. Eva was therefore appalled to find the same thing happening again the following month. So great had been her flow that she imagined her opening to be a wide one, like a huge river mouth. Not wide enough, though. On their wedding night he wasn't able to get into her. The trouble was that she had no idea at all about what was entailed, just some rather passionate kissing she supposed, and never really got over that initial shock of discovering that he had to put that huge dirty bit of him into her secret area. What was the point of all the pretty underwear – camisoles, French knickers, slips, all sewn and trimmed by hand – if not to hide the ugly bits underneath? Of course eventually he managed it, after making her drink several very large sherries, and in time it became simply another domestic duty to be ranked just above cleaning the toilet but never to be compared with ironing a nice pile of wind-fresh sheets. Years later when Caroline, their eldest daughter, talked about the pleasure involved in the act she experienced a surge of anger.

There were three girls rather than the one boy and one girl that they planned. After the second, she suffered a dark depression which baffled, embarrassed and finally enraged Richard.

'Life's too short!' he would say in frustration, 'Too short to be bloody miserable. You're a long time dead! Cheer up, Evie. It's not that bad.'

Once again her body betrayed her and though, in his own way, Richard carried on loving her she took his sense of her failure and buried it deep inside. She contemplated suicide then and even half-heartedly swallowed a few aspirin but managed to sleep the effects off without anyone ever knowing. Other methods – car, knife, rope – scared her, so instead one Saturday night she deliberately didn't insert her cap. A third baby, another beautiful one too, but a girl and after that she gave up.

Just come to give your locker a bit of a clear out, Eva. Are these all your family, Eva? Aren't they a bonny lot? I bet they'll be missing you at home?

'Like hell.' Eva's blistered lips attempt to shape an answer.

Of course they will. Bye for now, love.

Does she believe in Hell and if so is she going there? Or perhaps this is it, the not dying, the being here, the refusal of the body to do the decent thing. Cells have a death wish, she read once, and it's only the messages from other surrounding cells that tell them to struggle on. She is in a cell now, the white room with the dusty spider plant on the window sill, a *Now Wash Your Hands* sign over the basin and *Get Well Soon* cards pinned to a cork board above her bed and so only visible upside down in the mirror opposite.

She watches her visitors from behind half-lidded eyes, embarrassed as they attempt to negotiate the small wheelie thing at the left hand side of her bed from which hangs a pouch of her thick warm urine and the stand on her other side with a bag of someone else's blood suspended from it. They are variously impatient, bored and, sometimes, upset. She watches them read her charts, her cards, hold her hand, look out of the window, stroke her forehead, look at their watches, arrange the flowers and eat the food they'd brought and, on one occasion, go through the contents of her handbag. She feels no animosity at the latter.

'Go ahead, take anything you want!' she wants to cry out.

Instead she gurgles.

Richard used to say, 'Life's there for the taking, Evie! Nothing ventured, nothing gained! You make your own

43

opportunities in this world, they won't come looking for you.'

Not that he was inclined to let her out into the big, bad world. Her job was to raise the girls and look after the home and, if she was honest, she'd been clappy to do that. No, not clappy. Happy. Happy-clappy. Fuck religion. Eva, really! *Happiness, happiness* – a song by that comedian. Who was he? Richard, who was that comedian with strange hair who sang about being happy?

She can sense that Caroline is the one who is most strung out, rushing in after work and in her lunch hour sometimes bringing one of the children with her, pressing them towards the bed to kiss grandma while they, poor mites, shrink from this alien with papery skin who is operated by a bank of machines.

'Take them to the park, for God's sake, take them into the fresh air. Please.' she begs with a flicker of an eyelid.

She yearns for a cigarette, even when they decide her lungs aren't working anymore and attach her to a machine that appears to be a kind of electronic bellows. The first suck on a cigarette, that's all she longs for – when the filter is still dry, firm and unstained, when you take a long draw, swallow the smoke and feel it pushing down into the fretwork of bronchial tubes, when the racing of the heart is eased and a wonderful peace descends. She dreams of other newnesses – of a much anticipated book, pages still stiff and cover shiny, of the crocus bulbs in her window box waiting to thrust their tips through the dark soil, of the unopened bottle of Harvey's Bristol Cream in her bedside cupboard at home, sunrise, birthdays, the first apple blossom, the return of her favourite drama serial, a stack of unopened Christmas cards, the first fall of snow, the sense of surprise – shock, joy or fear – that can still pierce through the deterioration of the flesh like a shaft of light.

With a jolt, she remembers the tune.

Renal failure, I'm afraid, with probable permanent damage to the brain stem, though we have no real way of knowing. It's your choice.

She's always resented the way choices have been made for her, by her mother, by Richard and, latterly, by the children. But now, with a gradual sinking, a not unpleasurable sense of drowning in herself, of her body being pulled deep down into the bed while something else struggles to break the surface for air, she isn't able to blame them for making choices about quality of life even if it is their own rather than hers.

The faint, sweet sounds of music are returning like silver drops of rain and for that she offers them only thanks.

Not long now.

Smiling, she again offers her hand, milky-white skin in black silk, and feels it gently taken.

Words, Words, Words

'AHMAD! THAT WILL not do! It is very important that you look ... poor. Perhaps a bit ... dirtier. Do you understand?'

Frank enunciated each word slowly, speaking firmly as to a child. Ahmad watched his lips and wondered at the stream of incomprehensible sounds that they emitted. He knew that Frank was cross with him but not why. Then Frank jabbed a finger at Ahmad's chest making it obvious he thought the shirt was no good. But the shirt was new! The day before his landlady Bella had left a tray outside his room on which was the shirt and a cup of what he assumed was coffee. He shrugged his shoulders to show he didn't understand and Frank, turning away, began barking something into the phone that was clamped to his ear.

With the back of his hand Ahmad stroked the shirt, amazed once more by its softness. Monisha's hair had been soft. Soft and smoothly brown like a pelt. Every evening he would call her and she would run to sit at his feet, so close that he could feel the heat of the day radiating from her. How he marvelled at all that knowledge inside her head! He used to cup his hand over that delicate, fine-boned skull and then gently run his palm down over her hair. Sometimes the rough skin on his hand would catch and snag it and she would pull away in mock annoyance. Now, after just a week in the United States of America, he noticed how that rough skin was softening. In fact there was so much hot water that his fingertips were turning pulpy.

Frank was getting more agitated, 'We have a Press Call with all the major networks at four, Ahmad. Say, has your beard been trimmed?'

He peered at Ahmad and then swatted vaguely at him with one hand as if he was a troublesome fly before returning to pacing up and down the room. Why are you so angry, Ahmad wanted to ask. At first he had thought it was to do with Monisha's death. Now he wasn't so sure.

'President Obama?' Ahmad enquired tentatively to the back of Frank's bullet shaped head. He wasn't sure if he'd pronounced the words correctly.

Frank swung round, surprised.

'President Obama?' Ahmad repeated, knowing he sounded like the stupid peasant farmer he was.

He could see the effort Frank made to contort his face into a smile. 'Yes, yes, all in good time. You don't need to say anything at the Press Conference. Not that you can anyway. Just repeat Monisha's name.' He mimed keeping the mouth shut.

Ahmad caught the word Monisha and sprang to catch it and hold it, fluttering, inside his cupped hands.

Monisha.

Rameen, his eldest son, had run to fetch him from the fields and at first all he could see was a heap of splintered wood, like a pyre, and pieces of paper blowing about in the gritty, desert wind. As he drew nearer, he saw her bag of books splattered like cockroaches under a man's boot. Then he saw her arm sticking out from under the pyre, a slim olive skinned arm with a silver band encircling the wrist. Bowing his head he wept while paper flapped around the two of them like birds' wings.

A few days later Frank came to the village in a jeep owned by one of the many Aid organisations. Through a translator he explained how Monisha had been hit by a crate dropped from an American plane; how this was an outrage and should be brought to the attention of the world. His organisation would pay for Ahmad to travel to the USA and put his case to President Obama himself. At first, sunk in grief, Ahmad wasn't interested in what this red-faced American was saying. It was Rameen who claimed that family honour demanded redress. Wouldn't Monisha have wanted her father to pursue the perpetrators of her unlawful killing? Actually, Ahmad wasn't convinced that Monisha would have done. He could picture her giving that lop-sided smile as if to say 'Do whatever you want to do but don't use me as an excuse.' At fifteen years old she had a clear-sighted and fierce independence which she had somehow achieved without ever undermining his authority. Her winning a scholarship to the High School was a cause for celebration by the whole village and Rameen, skilled with words, had managed to convince their community that it was right for her father to make the trip. Without a full night's sleep since Monisha's death, Ahmad's bones ached from exhaustion. He offered little resistance.

'You OK, Ahmad buddy?' Frank was asking. His face shone with sweat and he kept trying to loosen the tie that was knotted round his fat neck. He gave a questioning thumbs up.

Ahmad returned the thumbs up gesture.

On their way from the airport Ahmad had gazed out of the window and wondered at the city of his country's liberators, so often described to them as one of riches and unbounded prosperity. It was true enough. Not only was there an infinite supply of everything but it was all so big: the food portions, the buildings and even the people themselves. Massive words shouted down at him from hoardings the size of small mountains; on some there were flashing lights, on others pictures of beautiful shameless women and men with orange bodies and shining, white teeth. Of course he recognised some of the symbols – McDonalds, Coca Cola – but the rest became a welter of colour and movement that made his head hurt.

What he had never expected to see were beggars slumped on street corners or drunks, women as well as men. He'd even seen a man urinate on the street in broad daylight. What was most shocking was the way that the black men sweeping the streets, washing cars or working in the toilets, kept their eyes cast down as if their jobs had no dignity. Was President Obama, a black man himself with two black daughters, not interested in this?

The Press Conference was a blitz of exploding lights and shouting which reminded Ahmad of an airstrike. The microphone heads that were thrust at them looked like grenades and it was difficult not to flinch as Frank answered questions. Behind them was an enlarged photograph of Monisha. Ahmad was glad he didn't have to sit facing it; Monisha looked very, very lovely and the picture gave him a pain in his heart.

He didn't hear from Frank all that day or the following one, so stayed inside with Bella and her son Jerry who was a little simple and had a belly like an oversized gourd. Ahmad liked the way the three of them ate together, smoked, watched television and communicated with a combination of mime, hand gestures and the little English he had acquired. It reminded him of sitting around the village fire, talking the sort of meandering, aimless talk that was not remembered in the morning but after which lingered a rich, grainy residue of comradeship.

More days passed and still no Frank. Every morning on waking Ahmad took his plane ticket out and checked the date and time of his return flight. Reassured, he would then say his prayers, kneeling on the towel Bella had kindly provided. Then he would make his way downstairs to the family room where the rest of the day would be spent in front of the giant television screen.

Bella liked the shows where real people got angry with each other, shouting and screaming, while someone in charge tried to sort it out, just like the elders did back home. Jerry preferred cartoons and Ahmad found he also enjoyed watching animals being flattened under car wheels and dropped from great heights but then quickly returning to their original shape. Sometimes one of the news channels would be showing a film of his country, or at least one very like it: men marching with guns along mountain tracks and tanks rolling down the main street of a big city while helicopters circled overhead. Bella and Jerry soon realised that watching that kind of thing made him sad and changed channels by pointing the controller at the screen and taking aim as if it was a gun and the screen was a target.

One afternoon Ahmad was slumped in a chair, watching the television through half closed eyes. The volume was always turned up but Ahmad had learned to tolerate the clamour, even starting to find it strangely soothing. Then suddenly, amidst the blur of moving images, he spotted a familiar figure and sat up, shocked.

It was Frank.

He was standing on a platform with other men at

some kind of meeting. There was a crowd listening to him while he ranted and threw his arms around. Some of the people carried placards with a picture of President Obama that had been altered to give him horns or a neat black moustache. The camera zoomed in on someone who was dressed in an ape costume but who also wore a mask of the President's face. Every so often Frank would invite a response from his audience and they would cheer but not in a good way. Ahmad knew that they were a mob and Frank was a leader who was wanting them to do bad things. Although Ahmad could not understand what was being said, hadn't he seen enough in his own country of the same kind of thing? Of men who rode into their village in trucks, making all sorts of promises to them as long as they voted the right way, promises that everyone knew they could never deliver.

Suddenly Ahmad experienced a stab of remorse so acute that his hand involuntarily went to his chest. He realised then that he had handed over Monisha's memory to a stranger, someone who was most probably a bad man. Somehow Frank had used his daughter as nothing more than a weapon for a cause of which he, Ahmad, was ignorant. She had become a victim and Monisha, his darling headstrong girl, could never be that. Worst of all her own father, whose duty it was to protect her, had colluded in this happening. Now he needed to be home: home where Monisha would be remembered not as a picture but as a real girl who sometimes bickered with Rameen, sulked about looking after the little ones and who had started to be vain about her beautiful hair; where stories would be told by those who knew her in words that made sense. He started crying, great raw sobs tearing at his throat which started Jerry crying and then Bella.

Ahmad flew home three days later, with still no contact from Frank. In his pocket was the one remaining leaflet from the crate, now crumpled and torn. He had memorised its words. What offended him most was not the message itself, exhorting his people to stand strong against the rebels and to work with the occupying forces. Propaganda and politics went hand in hand – even the simplest goatherd knew that. His country had been at war for so many years and its history was a history of wars. No, what offended him most was the quality of the words. The gist of the translation was clear but the cadences, rhythm and beauty of his language had been casually butchered.

Monisha had always been particular with words, choosing each one carefully like one would smooth pebbles to skim over water. It was Rameen and the other young men who talked fast and furiously, repeating words they'd heard preached and chanting slogans. Monisha had been killed because someone somewhere thought that words could make a difference. And maybe they could, thought Ahmad, as he stepped off the plane and stood at the top of the steps, dry heat smacking him in the face. President Obama must have a fine way with words. He had watched the ceremony when Obama was made president and he'd seen many people in the crowd with tears of joy rolling down their faces.

Ahmad pulled up the top edge of his *chapan* to cover his nose and mouth from the fine grit in the air but not before he had breathed in roasting lamb, petrol fumes and human stink. Then, putting his bag down bedside him, he reached into the folds of his garment and closed his fingers over the pieces of paper there. In one movement he brought his clenched fists to shoulder height and, like a magician releasing doves, opened his hands. What remained of the leaflet found near Monisha's body mixed with subway receipts and chewing gum wrappers in a fluttering whorl before it drifted down and settled into the dust. A gentle touch to his elbow indicated that other passengers were waiting for him to disembark. Carefully holding the handrail, Ahmad started his descent. Shading his eyes he thought he could make out the small figure of Rameen standing with his face pressed against the glass of the viewing lounge looking for his father.

Grains of Truth

THE VICTIM

She's often imagined her funeral, hoped that the church would be packed, standing room only, and that people would queue up to say lovely things about her. But never this – the actual dying bit. Face down with her head to one side, she watches as blood, her blood, pools then drains into the sand, staining it pink. She hears the screech of a seagull but maybe it's her own voice from minutes before still trapped in the space between the cliffs and the sea. The small blade glinted in the late evening sun and after the horror of the first blow she felt nothing. The water is licking her hair and gradually she senses it loosening from her scalp. With each wave the sea creeps in under her body, gently shifting it. As her mouth fills and her brain empties, she wishes only to be turned on her back so that the last thing she sees is sky.

FIRST ON THE SCENE

I'm on the beach. OK not a beach in the sense of seaside – candy floss, donkey rides, amusements. This is Spurn Point: a long strip of land curling into the North Sea. It's November – a cold, grey afternoon with a bitter easterly wind and I'm walking away my grief. Or rather trying to. I have the beach to myself: nobody else is crazy enough to be out here.

From a distance it looks like a big pile of seaweed, just a huddle of dark stuff at the water's edge. Drawing nearer I can make out something patterned: whatever it is must have been washed up by the tide. Above me the sky yawns huge and empty and the wind shrieks in my ears: I started off with a scarf wrapped round my head but it kept slipping off so I knotted it round my neck and now it streams behind like a Biggles cartoon. He loved it here, loved the emptiness, the bigness of the sky and the fact that we seemed powerless against the elements. In recent years the spit has fractured and all along this stretch of the north east coast houses are falling into the sea; in some strange way he admired the relentless erosion, Nature rebutting his work as an architect. This place is where he proposed, thirty-two years ago, and where he chose to tell me about his cancer. He shouldn't have done that, polluting our special place.

When I am within about six feet, I get the first inkling of what is lying on the sand but at first I refuse to acknowledge it. I'm very aware of being consumed by death at the moment. Only when my feet are inches from what lies there do I have to accept that this was once a living human being. With shaking hands I get out my mobile. At my side the water scrolls angrily and sucks at my shoes.

THE SUSPECT

He's never been in trouble. Never ever. Not even a detention in school and certainly nothing afterwards. Getting a library fine (it only happened once and that was because he had a migraine and couldn't summon the energy to pick up the phone to renew) upset him not because of the money but because people at the library might think he was untrustworthy. When his Mum says the police are downstairs he's so scared he craps himself. The time it takes to get cleaned up and change his underwear and trousers must look suspicious, as if perhaps he is trying to destroy evidence. Then all their questions confuse and panic him and he contradicts himself. When they say he's going to be taken to the police station it isn't a surprise.

THE DETECTIVE

Another loser by the look of it. He might as well have murderer stamped on his bloody forehead. They're always so pathetic in the flesh. We'll have to go through the whole rigmarole of getting hold of the duty solicitor, setting up the interview, asking a load of questions and listen to him repeating 'No comment' without reacting even when you feel like smashing a fist into his stupid face. Probably should get him medically assessed before we start: he looks like one of those fragile little flowers who will pull any trick in the book to avoid facing up to what they've done. Innocent until proven guilty. Yeah, right. He's been in a relationship with the victim, pretty one-sided by all accounts, and there's witnesses who can confirm they had a row at lunchtime on the day in question as a result of which he got really upset. Then there's the fact that he can't account for his whereabouts for two hours of that afternoon and we've found sand and blood stains in his car. Just waiting for forensics to get back to us about the knife found in the sand dunes not far from the body: it's a small kitchen one like you'd use for vegetables and matches initial assessments of the weapon used to inflict the fatal wounds. An open and shut case, take my word for it.

THE VICTIM'S MOTHER

She used to tease me about my addiction. My favourites were *Happy Valley* and *Broadchurch* but I also liked Scandinavian series like *The Bridge*. I was a sucker for any crime drama. But that was then. I don't put the telly on now, not even for the news. Everything out there appals me. Don't get me wrong – people have been wonderful: kind, generous, thoughtful. They've sent flowers, cards, little notes and my fridge is stocked with meals. But I just want to scream at them to fuck off and I'm not someone who ever swears normally. This is not normal, though. My beautiful girl, who loved attention and lit up any room she walked into, was left to die alone and without dignity on a cold, empty beach. Her father was already upset by my call the night before. When I break the news he goes to pieces and I'm the one who has to keep it together. It's always been the other way round so that's something else that makes the world tip further out of kilter. I feel an unexpected wash of tenderness for him: we've now been divorced for longer than we were together and I've forgotten how he can be moved. When we first met he was a passionate, jealous man but that soon faded once his career took off and he started making serious money. She's a Daddy's girl. Was. I don't think I will ever get used to using the past tense.

I know some people think I'm a hard-hearted bitch. That I've become that way to succeed in a man's world. Bollocks. The way I look at it, I am how I am because that's the way to get cases solved as quickly and efficiently as possible. Success in my terms is simple: it's taking villains off the streets, putting them away for as long as possible, so making the world just a little bit safer. Am I upset at seeing the body of a lovely young woman who's been murdered in broad daylight? No, not upset: just determined to nail the bastard who did it.

My own daughter was killed – by meningitis, aged three – and there was no one I could pin that on.

THE SUSPECT

When the duty desk sergeant tells him why they've brought him in for questioning, the floor slips away from under his feet and two policemen have to hold him up although in one sense he knew she was already lost to him. It's a wonder they lasted as long as they have – four months and nine days – and he's always known the end must come sooner or later. As everyone was quick to point out, she was out of his league: above average in the looks department, a graduate who'd landed, with Daddy's help, an exciting job that involved travel and smart living. By contrast he's been in the same job at the Co-op bank since leaving school and as for his dad, he never knew him. Buggered off before he was born. Yet here's the thing: he and his girlfriend (what a tang of pleasure that word still gives!) found something special.

Away from everyone else she's different: quieter and more thoughtful. They talk for hours, often while walking on beaches along this stretch of the coast, and she tells him things she said she's never told anybody before. They lean into one another, her long hair blowing across his face. He loves the fresh shampoo smell of her hair.

FIRST ON THE SCENE

The family liaison officer arranges for me to visit the victim's mother and give an account of how I found her daughter's body. I'm nervous, obviously, but also glad to think that I may be of help. I've already decided to give a slightly edited version of events, to dwell on the stark beauty of the surroundings rather than the state of the body itself. I needn't have worried. The meeting is a waste of time: I don't think the poor woman is even aware of what I'm saying as she clutches a photo of her daughter's graduation to her chest. The father is present and is more in control. He thanks me for coming, offers a cup of coffee and makes general chit chat. After about twenty minutes he indicates, very nicely and tactfully, that it's best for me to go.

People say that if you've never had children, then you can't appreciate the pain of losing one. Certainly there's no way I can compare her bereavement with mine and say which is worse. But then again that makes me angry. Surely loss is loss, whoever it is?

Forensics report that the blood from the car is his. Not a trace of hers. We ask him how it got there and he claims he cut himself. Shows us the marks, which look newly inflicted, and his mother confirms a history of self-harm. But good news on the knife – it's confirmed both as his and as the murder weapon. We've still got enough to charge him I reckon.

THE VICTIM'S MOTHER

Her Dad moves back in temporarily, just until after the funeral he says, and he's a great support. Manages visitors, fields phone calls, cooks and cleans, looks after me. I believe a few eyebrows are raised, and at one time that would have bothered me but not now. He's the only other person in the world I want around. The two of us made her, so it's fitting that the two of us share the pain of losing her. In the evenings we look at old photo albums: pictures of her newly born, in the pram in the garden, later as a toddler on the beach. She always loved the beach. How about that for an irony?

Of course in recent times photos were stored on my laptop. The month before she and her boyfriend went to Scotland for a few days and she sent me some lovely pictures of the two of them: climbing Ben Nevis, striking funny poses at Loch Ness, on the ferry to Skye. They made a good looking couple: it was only when you got to know the lad that you became aware of a softness about his features and a certain … I don't know how to put this … weakness of character. But I liked him. He gave me to understand his own Mum was a bit flaky so I became a kind of stand-in.

My ex-husband flinches when I open the folder with the Scotland photos. Then he reaches over me and closes it. His lips are tight and a muscle in the corner of his eye twitches. He's always made it clear he disapproves of this latest relationship although he struggles to justify his view given that she's had a string of highly undesirable boyfriends, into drink and drugs and all sorts, and at least here is someone with a steady job who clearly worships the ground she walks on.

THE SUSPECT

He hates rows – always has done. He'll walk away if someone tries to have a go at him. Turn the other cheek and all that. The day started off well. After exchanging texts during the course of the morning, they arrange to meet for lunch near his office, she insisting on an expensive place rather than their usual cafe. As he watches her sashay towards the table, attracting admiring glances as she does so, not for the first time he can't believe his good luck. As they eat, she seems a bit on edge, the reason for this becoming clear when at the end of the meal she produces, with a flourish, a small velour box. Even without opening it, he knows it will be an engagement ring. Not only does he delight in these kind of surprises, she is used to getting her own way. And she wants marriage.

He doesn't – not yet anyway. It's too much too soon and the thought of rushing things makes his insides clench with anxiety. Apart from potential problems about where they will live (she's made it very clear she wants it to be abroad) there's his Mum to consider, who he thinks might be going a bit funny in the head. Of course he completely messes up his response, all the words come out wrong, and she goes ballistic, throwing the ring on the floor and storming out of the restaurant. He's blown it and nobody, least of all him, will ever be able to understand why.

Once he's back at the bank he shuts himself in the toilet, rolls up his sleeve and with great care cuts himself on both forearms with the small knife he always keeps in the inside pocket of his suit jacket. Then he tells reception he has a migraine coming on and needs to go home, looking so pale that nobody doubts him. Once out of the city he feels ill and has to pull in to a layby. Turning off the engine, he leans his head on the wheel and as he does so feels the small reassuring nudge of the knife in his inside pocket. It's like an old friend. He takes it out and places it on the passenger seat, then shrugs off his jacket and rolls up his sleeves. The wounds are still bloody but only superficial: in time they will heal and become part of the network of scars and ridges that fretwork his skin. Physically he will survive: it's the shame and self-loathing which always threaten to tip him over.

On impulse, he decides to phone her Mum to explain what happened at lunchtime. The two of them get on well and there was another occasion when he enlisted her help to sort out a misunderstanding. It must be because his hands are shaking but by mistake he calls her Dad on Speed Dial and finds himself blurting out the whole sorry story. Surprisingly her Dad is sympathetic, saying he is grateful to be told. 'Don't you worry, son,' he says, 'You just stay where you are. I'll come over and sort it.' It's nice to be called 'son'.

Within an hour her Dad arrives during which time he sits there numbly, unable to summon the energy to roll down his sleeves or conceal the knife. With a quick glance her Dad takes it all in but doesn't comment; he insists on driving him home and says one of his staff will retrieve his own vehicle later in the day. A dreamless sleep engulfs him for the rest of the afternoon and it's the police knocking at the door and his Mum calling that wakes him up and the real nightmare begins.

THE VICTIM'S MOTHER

My daughter was not a very nice person. It doesn't mean I loved her any less or grieve any less now she's dead. None of us are perfect but my daughter was selfish, vain and ruthless: in that respect she took after her father though she also had his charm and passion for life. In the past he's always eventually managed to persuade her to dump a boyfriend he didn't deem good enough for his little Princess. Threats, bribes, ridicule, careful argument – he'd use all the tools at his disposal. But he couldn't seem to manage it with this one. The night before she rang me to say they were getting engaged and begged me to tell her Dad. When I did so the line went dreadfully silent and I knew that he was beyond angry.

It's not that I suspect him of being involved, that would be completely unthinkable, but I wonder if I should speak to someone – perhaps the nice family liaison officer.

At first I can't explain how the knife got on the beach. Then I realise who might have taken it there. I imagine a fight: they were a father and daughter who both knew exactly which buttons to press and perhaps she told him that I know their little secret. Know how he treated her as a child. Not strictly abuse, she insisted, not really. Just what might today be termed 'inappropriate'. There'd been no touching, not for years, but he still liked to keep her close.

My solicitor tells me her father's denying ever seeing me that afternoon and maybe he didn't. I think possibly I did kill her and have managed to blank it from my mind. Craziness – maybe it's in the genes. I don't care now anyway. Without her I'm like a speck of sand that has been ground into nothingness. In my dreams the two of us walk on and on over endless beaches but when I dare to turn around and look back our footprints have been obliterated. I don't know whether this is because they have been washed away or because we did not exist. When I wake I can sometimes smell her hair and taste the salt on her skin.

I'll do anything to stop all the questions.

THE DETECTIVE

Something doesn't feel quite right about this case but today the lad comes as near as damn it to confessing. He's in a terrible state so we won't be able to do much more with him. But here's another strange thing – this morning as he shuffles out of the interview room I am suddenly struck by a realisation so strong I have to grab on to the table edge for support: this lad is somebody's child and long ago his mother will have held him in her arms and promised to protect him from the world. But just like me she failed. From now on his world will be unbearably brutal and I know he is unlikely to survive. At the same time, another bit of my brain is telling me I should have had some breakfast, especially after a heavy night. Telling myself to get a grip, I bark at my colleague to stop fucking gawping, get off his fat arse and ring the duty medic.

THE VICTIM'S MOTHER

I like him being here in the house. It's as if I was never allowed to have both of them at once. At least now I'm not alone and we can remember together. I've told the police that I don't need the family liaison officer any more.

FIRST ON THE SCENE

I see the parents of the dead girl in town. It's late night shopping and the place is heaving, what with Christmas only a fortnight away. I'm not sure it's them at first. They're walking closely together, his arm round her shoulder guiding her through the crowd. There's nothing to suggest what they've suffered recently, not only their daughter's death but the fact that she was murdered by her boyfriend. (I hear on the grapevine that he's been declared unfit to stand trial and is being held in a secure hospital.) I understood her parents were divorced so maybe the tragedy has brought them back together. In fact they could be any middle aged couple picking up the last few bits and bobs for the grandchildren and although I know that in their case there never can be any grandchildren I must admit I envy them their closeness, their companionship. After all, isn't that what everyone wants? Somebody to be at your side so you're not walking by the water alone.

Beneath the Skin

OVER THE YEARS I have met many people and been witness to many events. Age brings wisdom, so they say, but I'd take issue with that. In some ways I feel as ignorant now as when I first came into being. And again they get it wrong: ignorance is not bliss. It is fear. So what *do* I know, you ask. I know that people are basically the same, that fine clothes and fancy manners cannot disguise greed and envy but neither are patched, threadbare garments any guarantee of virtue. Skin is skin and beneath it the same organs throb and pulse to keep blood pumping around the body.

In my prime, I was hospitable and threw open my doors to all those who society deemed the good and the great. They'd come for a walk around my grounds then take a cup of China tea under the great oak, whiling away the hours with light conversation that reassured them of everything in the world being safe and comfortable; or they'd do business, haggling about costs and profits, fretting about the risks in importing cedar from India, downing schooners of sherry while the air grew sticky with argument. I used to be particular, not just about who came but how they behaved when they did. I believed that there was a right way of doing things and a wrong way. But in time I learnt the foolishness of fighting against the tide of change and with age grew more relaxed. I mellowed and embraced anyone who came with good intent.

Now, at night, when my rooms are empty and I feel hollowed out through loneliness, I sometimes think about all those who have met, become friends, maybe even found love within my walls and wish that I could ask them all back and have a grand ball as in the old days: a chandelier darting shards of light onto the dancers' heads below, shoes tap tapping on the polished floor, the swish of dresses, clink of glasses and music, always music; on summer nights, laughter tumbled out onto the lawn and cigarettes glowed like fireflies. Yet it is the way of the world that some of those people who danced, laughed and kissed will also have fought and wounded one another; that in the darkness of the woodland beyond the lawn dreadful things will have happened.

Remembering those grand occasions I am often left afterwards with a feeling of great weariness. All that time and effort expended on what proved to be so ephemeral: the morning afterwards just the faintest aroma of claret and cigars lingering in the dining room, perfume and talcum powder in the drawing room; a single, splayed glove on the chest in the entrance hall and a smear of mud on the tiles are the only signs that for those few hours we existed inside the fragile skin of a rainbow coloured bubble. Today those bright young things will be as old as I am and I can't help wondering how much they care to remember of the time when they blossomed like exotic hothouse plants, some basking in the heat while others, overshadowed by their more showy friends, wilted almost immediately. There will be those who will want to forget the frenzy that phase of their lives engendered while others will perhaps mourn its loss. Maybe that's dependant on how much time they now have for daydreams: whether grandchildren snuggle on their laps or whether that place is reserved for a cat. Does the gentle touch of a loved one's hand against the cheek serve to make the past less important? Or when the only touch is that of a cool breeze on a solitary walk is it inescapable that thoughts will drift backwards? A lot of them will be dead of course. As I've got older I've seen less of people. I'm shabbier, duller, less attractive. I can't hold sway like I used to and in some ways I don't want to. Everything has its time and I'm sad but not bitter when I say that mine has come and gone. There are paintings and photographs which claim to capture a moment but you cannot record life, only live it. The present instantly becomes the past and looking back can be dangerous: like a cracked mirror it can distort reality. Many faces and names I cannot recall, while some I cannot forget.

Lady B. A regular guest who swanned in as if she was royalty, looking down her thin nose at everyone, her beady eyes searching for dust, a wrongly placed piece of cutlery, a head not dipped low enough to show due deference. Of course everyone knew that Lord B was a philanderer and that she was dependant upon him for her privileged lifestyle. Only I knew that after her maid had left at night she would tear at her hair in frustration and slam her hands into the bedpost again and again until they bled. She bit her nails to the quick, always wore gloves. And what of that maid who backed out of the best bedchamber with a small curtsey and a 'Goodnight Madam' to Lady B? She glowed with a secret: that she was in love with a young man who worked in another big house nearby, who loved her with equal passion. She could put up with the indignities of her job, the slopping out and her mistress's rank body odour, for as long as it took to save up enough money to be wed. However, I have also learnt that this smug moral equation (rich = unhappy, poor = happy) is often disproved by life. I'm sorry to report that the maid's young man proved in time to be a gambler and a loser, abandoning her to raise their three children on a pittance while he sought to make his fortune in Canada.

John. I will call him that, though it was not his given name. A faithful servant for many years, he started as a junior footman and ended up being almost one of the family. Long after the very idea of having footmen seemed incredible, John played a discrete but vital role in the household. Whatever needed doing – driving, fetching supplies, organising domestic repairs, chaperoning the ladies – John was our man. He even had his bedroom on the first floor and that is where he hanged himself from the light fitting with his belt. His body was discovered swaying gently in the draught like some monstrous flower. John was dressed in his old livery, which nobody knew still existed, his face was purple, his eyes bulged and his swollen tongue lolled out of his mouth like the tongue of a shoe. He had emptied his bladder and bowels, at least that's what everyone said. That same everyone knew he liked young boys but I was never aware of him doing anything more than looking and stealing the occasional furtive embrace. But one little lad from the village with an eye on the main chance said he'd done a lot more and this lad's father was on the warpath. As I said, John was almost one of the family but that word 'almost' is key here. Once the body was cut down and removed, the family ensured that they washed their hands of him as thoroughly as they ordered the floorboards that had absorbed his bodily excretions to be scrubbed.

So many others. Jane died of scarlet fever, aged six, closely followed by three of her siblings. Her mother ended up in an asylum; Robert became one of the country's top lawyers, often defending paupers for nothing; Elijah tried to set the place on fire while under the influence; Mrs Bentley, the cook, lived until the ripe old age of ninety three and went on producing her famous Yorkshire puddings right up until the week before she died; Alexandria, the girl who should have been a boy; Thomas invented a new kind of loom that made him a fortune; Miss Prendle survived The Titanic, an event which came to define her; Maud was a suffragette and smoked black cigarettes; Samuel lost everything in The Wall Street Crash though you'd never have known it by his ever-cheerful demeanour; although never achieving the Hollywood stardom she craved, Rachel did become a film actress; Richard, call me Rick, went to India and came back a Buddhist, erecting shrines in the by then unkempt garden; Sally the dot com entrepreneur; Shane the Greenpeace activist; Mark the property developer; Grace a finalist in *Britain's Got Talent* (she and her pet goat did Zumba together).

I remained here through two world wars and God knows how many other smaller but no less bloody conflicts in the years since. Men went away to serve their country and of the lucky ones who came back most returned to their old jobs – but they were never the same. With some the change was obvious, a missing limb or a badly burnt face, while others seemed unmarked although those hidden wounds were often far worse. Something else was different: difficult to put your finger on but an attitude, a way of thinking. As if nothing was permanent and that if we were capable of ripping the heart out of Europe and soaking its fields with the blood of our young men then nothing had intrinsic value anymore. Over time the weaponry and means of transportation changed and what was actually happening in the war zones became clearer but the reasons for the slaughter remained as murky as ever. Men never seem to lose the urge to butcher one another and I don't pretend to understand it. Watch little boys at play and you'll see their murderous instincts as sticks transmute into swords or guns. Girls are not immune, of course, but they tend towards using words rather than fists. At the time just as hurtful and often slower to heal.

So if you were expecting a philosophy of life from someone as old as me I'm afraid you will be disappointed. As the sun rises and bathes my bricks with warmth I stretch, my joints creaking. I'm always grateful, and a little surprised, still to be standing. My facade is crumbling, my doors and window frames are brittle bones and in one place my roof gapes to the heavens like an open wound; birds nest in my timbers and throughout my rooms and corridors rats reign supreme, bloated oligarchs. Inside layers of wallpaper peel, flayed skin, and damp patches are like bruises. No longer serving any purpose, I am a burden and that hurts. Those visiting now will remark, with what they assume to be sparkling originality, 'If only houses could speak, what stories they could tell'. Indeed. Others will try and find out everything they can about me as if by doing so they can create order in their own lives and make sense of it all. And finally the men with hard hats and clipboards will come, stretching out yellow marker tape as if for a crime scene, which in a way it is.

Although some will try and save me, indeed they might well succeed in granting me a temporary reprieve and shoring me up for a little while longer, eventually the end will arrive. I have had my glory days and I rejoice in them. A house keeps the souls of those who have lived there in its DNA so that when I am stripped and gutted and reduced to dust I know that those souls will soar up into the sky, like a flock of starlings, higher and higher until they become barely visible specks in the distance. But still there if you look hard enough.

A Bench and a Ladder

'MOVE THE CANCER Bench for Chrissake!' I yelled through the kitchen window at Sam's back.

'Mum…' Flora said reproachfully, a frown pleating her pale forehead as she pushed chunks of pepper, courgette and mushroom onto skewers. She had cut them into equally sized pieces and lined them up in military rows on the worktop.

'Just shove it up against the wall, then we can get the other chairs round the table!'

'I'm busy, just in case you hadn't noticed!' Sam shouted over his shoulder. 'These chicken portions are taking bloody ages. Lads, get off your lazy arses and shift the bench will you!'

I watched as Robbie and his mate Danny remained on the loungers, twitching to music pounding through their ear buds. Then I bellowed, 'And remember not to let Flora's veggie burger touch the real ones!'

'Do you two have to shout all the time? And you shouldn't call it that,' Flora said.

'Call what what?'

'You know, the bench. The C word.'

'For fuck's sake, Flora!'

'Swearbox. One pound for the f word. That's what we agreed.'

'You agreed – I don't remember doing so. Anyway, why shouldn't I call it the *Cancer* Bench if I want to?' I asked irritably as I dunked dirty plates in the sink and rinsed them under the tap. Flora was such a prissy little madam.

God knows how Sam and I managed to produce her.

'Because it's something I'd rather forget.'

'It wasn't a barrel of laughs for me. How long are you going to be faffing about with those kebabs?'

I'd spotted the bench at a local craft fair, somewhere that, as I said to Sam, under normal circumstances he wouldn't be seen dead at. He flinched at my choice of words. I also told him I was only killing time and he didn't appreciate that either. It was odd because neither of us has ever been coy about discussing and joking about the biggies: sex, religion, death. We've always made it a policy to talk openly in front of the kids even though it embarrassed them. But then again they're going to get embarrassed whatever we say. We've got Larkin's quote about your parents fucking you up in the downstairs loo and I've noticed that the kids always direct visitors to the upstairs one.

The seat of the bench was made out of solid wood – probably oak – a beautiful rich conker-brown buffed until it gleamed. I couldn't resist reaching out and placing my palm flat on its warm surface. Although we already had plenty of garden chairs, not to mention a swing seat and the aptly named loungers, I had to have it. From that moment the word 'malignant' had entered our everyday vocabulary, almost three months previously, Sam could refuse me nothing and he eagerly handed over a wad of twenties as if by doing so he could buy my health. While we waited for the biopsy results, a matter of days, we were both aware of every minute of every hour. It wasn't that time stood still – more that every moment was imbued with a sense of significance. While cleaving together, we each dealt with the situation in our own way. Sam needed to make big gestures whereas with me it was mundane activities about which I agonised: whether to book the City Break that we took each Autumn or whether to get my winter coat dry cleaned. In three months' time I had an appointment for a full head of highlights: would there be any hair left to highlight?

'I'd get you the moon if I could find a long enough ladder,' Sam announced the evening before Judgement Day, 'I would you know. I bloody would.'

He had tears in his eyes and his hand shook as he raised a glass to his lips. To be fair, we had both consumed the best part of two bottles of Rioja and I told him not to be such a silly bugger. The next morning was a scorcher, the kind of day when, before our world had shifted on its axis, I would have rushed home from work to lie out on the back grass, feeling the heat flush my bare skin. Now the sun streaming through the thin bedroom curtains seemed to taunt us. We stumbled out of bed, heavy–headed, dressed and showered and went downstairs. Sam had insisted we didn't tell the kids about the significance of the day but they probably guessed what with their dad stopping off work and both of us being so nice to one another. Robbie even offered to stack the dishwasher, which was unheard of, but reassuringly Flora was her usual schoolmarmy self, pointing out how many units of alcohol we'd consumed the night before.

When it came to it, the verdict was swift. In fact, Dr Randall didn't need to say anything. From the moment I stepped inside the air-conditioned consulting room and felt the soft coolness of the air on my bare arms and saw the relaxation of the muscles around his mouth I knew I was in the clear. Apart from minor scarring under my arms where lymph glands had been removed and not being able to sunbathe, there would be nothing in my day-to-day existence to serve as a reminder. I'd like to say that because of my scare I valued life more, that Sam was more attentive, the kids more unselfish. But none of those things happened. It's like driving very carefully immediately after you've been done for speeding: you soon forget and drive as fast as you did before, perhaps even faster assuming that the odds on getting caught again have been reduced. As for the Cancer Bench at first it seemed important that it was looked after. I put an old motorbike cover of Sam's over it at night and gave it a rub down every day to get rid of splashes of bird shit and fallen leaves. Standing at the kitchen window, I could see its rich, nutty solidity, confirmation that nothing had changed after all.

But over the summer I forgot to put the cover on every night. After all, I told myself, the bench was hardy. A bit of rain wouldn't hurt and a quick wipe every few days should be enough to keep it looking alright. Routine reasserted itself: work, evening meetings, Friday pub quiz, Saturday night takeaway in front of the telly. The care I'd lavished on the bench seemed a bit OTT when none of our other furniture, garden or otherwise, got that amount of attention. In my few rare moments of reflection I mourned the passing of my cancer and I know how weird that sounds. More than weird. Perverse. I struggled to explain it to myself but it was something to do with the fact that for those limbo days, when Sam and I knew something that nobody else did, we lived in our own private bubble. It reminded me of the start of our relationship when his every touch, gesture and look meant something and I held my breath in case he didn't feel the same, fearing that we wouldn't last. Both times we spent hours lying face to face, tasting each other's breath, the sensual bordering on sexual, delaying the moment when our bodies would fuse, when the extraordinary became mundane.

That BBQ, in early September just before the kids went back to school, was the last one of the year. The whole country was enjoying an Indian summer, with temperatures still high but the leaves starting to turn. I was clearing up later that evening when I noticed a blemish on the bench. It was only a small pockmark but initially it did give me a shock because it looked very much like the first indication of my melanoma. Obviously a bird had pecked it or the mark had been made by a chip of gravel: only to be expected when something was left exposed to the elements. But within three weeks the seat had become scarred, its rich brownness patched with mottled grey, and by November it had acquired some kind of fungus growing inside it. Horrible alien-type tubers were forcing themselves up between the cracks in the wood. I couldn't bear to look at it and nagged Sam to get rid of what had become an eyesore.

'Just dump it? What a waste of money! I'll do it up when I've got the time.'

Of course he never did find the time. Neither of us did. We were back to chasing our tails, bickering about who was going to take which kid where. My cancer was consigned to family history. With kids you co-exist with crisis on a daily basis: Sam and I both worried about Flora's reluctance to engage socially. I'd spotted scratches on her arms which she claimed were from brambles on a cross-country run. Did the school even do cross-country? When I had a minute it was something I needed to investigate. Robbie, by contrast, seemed to be out all the time and I had my doubts about the company he was keeping. Already that term Danny had been excluded twice.

Not long after that I found another spot under my rib-cage. This one was bigger, angrier and less forgiving.

'You'll need a longer ladder,' I said to Sam after a visit to the hospital confirmed what I had already guessed. His face leached of colour and he suddenly looked old, like his Dad. He took my hands in his and stroked my cheek softly with the back of his finger.

'We need to talk about this,' he said.

'No,' I replied. 'I don't want to.'

That night I went out, as planned, to see a film with a couple of girlfriends. I didn't want to be cocooned in their sympathy so I didn't tell them anything, instead spending the time thinking about my funeral. Hopefully I had long enough to brief Sam on exactly what I wanted on the Big Day. Despite being an atheist, I felt only a church ceremony could convey the appropriate gravitas and poignancy. Definitely no flowers but which charity did I want to nominate? Naturally it would be packed out and I pictured Sam at the front, upright and act-ing strong. I wondered whether Robbie would agree to play a guitar solo. But for some reason I couldn't envisage Flora there. My baby.

Someone gave me a friendly nudge. The film was a comedy, a chick flick, crude and in your face and I laughed as loudly as the others as the protagonist, a bride to be, fell into a pile of shit as she got out of her horse drawn carriage and then, walking down the aisle, tripped and tore her dress. We all knew it would turn out well in the end.

When I got back home most of the house was in dark-ness, just a yellow glow seeping from behind the curtains in Flora's room. Robbie must still have been out. I stood on the doorstep, a huge basin of inky sky tipping over me, and from the garage heard the sound of something being attacked.

Splintering wood; the voice I knew and loved so dearly uttering a little gasp or cry each time he wielded what must have been an axe. As the blows increased in frequency, I pictured sweat beading on his upper lip, the flush around his neck, heard his breath issuing in short pants just as it did when he came and each time the blade fell and our bench was gouged and mutilated I wondered what would be inside when it finally cracked open.

Blue Sky Thinking

Maisie is 43 and lives in an old rectory in Shropshire with her daughter, Gilly, and Peregrine, her cat. Her work has been published in a wide variety of anthologies and magazines and she was once short-listed for a major prize. She gets her inspiration from the sea and loves writing at the kitchen table with Peregrine on her lap and Radio 4 in the background.

The bio wasn't all made up! Gilly and Peregrine are real enough though Gilly only nominally lives here. I've kept her bedroom the same and occasionally she flits back in between her foreign jaunts. Peregrine's a complete bastard and wouldn't sit on anyone's lap, least of all mine. I keep thinking I ought to poison him. Living in Shropshire and mentioning the sea was obviously bloody stupid whereas the bit about the rectory was an out and out porky: it just sounded right, shades of the Brontës and all that. As for R4, I can't stand it: all those pretentious middle class women yapping on about hot flushes and GM crops. But I do like the sea. In spite of everything.

I started writing in my teens – just the usual kind of self-obsessed drivel – and continued when I started work in the bakery section at Morrisons. My days were boring and my evenings empty so I wrote. Pornography, mostly, or what nowadays they call erotic fiction. Don't think that helped me in the romantic stakes: nobody I went out with could ever match up to those I created on the page. In my admittedly limited experience, blokes don't tend to have both a large brain and a large penis.

Then I thought I'd try and get published. By this time I'd abandoned porn (*Fifty Shades* having beaten me to it) and was writing travel stuff. Not that I'd ever travelled, except for a week in Benidorm with Mum and Dad which was a total disaster, but you can do a lot by copying and pasting from Wikipedia. I didn't get anywhere with that – obviously not my métier. About this time Mum persuaded the local vicar to publish one of my pieces 'Taking the Grim out of Grimsby' in the parish mag. Small fry, I know, but it was great to see my name in print and it spurred me on to try other forms.

Poetry seemed a better option because blank verse means you can call any group of words a poem. The other advantage was that I could write loads at one time. My record was 27 in one week. Three of my poems were published in an anthology by a company called *Write as Rain* which advertised at the back of one of my writing magazines. The book had a lovely cover, purple with gold embossed lettering, although I did have to pay the company to cover costs and it was horrendously expensive.

Shortly after that I met Don (both of whose major organs, contrary to his belief, were of average size), we got married and had Gilly. My writing was consigned to the back burner. I did enrol on a number of Creative Writing classes but they consisted mostly of women and we tended to talk about our families, though sometimes one of us would write something sad and we'd all cry.

The bit about being short-listed was true. Well, longlisted actually. I wrote a story about a day at the beach.

It was the first thing I'd ever done that felt as if it had to be written and then, when it was, somehow the words turned out to be in the right place and managed to say the right thing.

* * *

Entry: 849
Category: Short story
Title: Blue Sky
Word count: 1410

It was the last day of a fortnight's holiday in Cornwall, their first proper time away since having Tilly. The weather was flawless and Jess had never seen a sky so unrelentingly clear and blue. Tilly had lost her inner city pallor and was a delicious biscuity colour. At five she was happy to amuse herself in the nearby rock pools as long as she could see her parents. Jess was reading but the print was dark and blurry through her sunglasses and she kept drifting off, lulled by the swish and suck of water on sand; the thwack of a cricket ball; the screech of seagulls. At that moment she thought herself happy. Jon had just got a promotion at work and to celebrate they were planning to eat out so there'd be no having to cook on the small hob in their 'luxury' self-catering flat. The sun felt good on her skin and she patted her shoulder to make sure she wasn't burning.

Someone next to them turned up their music. It was Meat Loaf's 'Bat Out of Hell' which Jess really liked but even so … she would ask Jon to say something when he came back from his swim. He was good at things like that.

He never came back. After a while Jess walked to the

water's edge, shaded her eyes but couldn't see him. At that point she wasn't worried. Jon was a good swimmer and sometimes swam around the headland to the other bay. Another hour of pacing up and down the shoreline and then she did panic. Calling to Tilly so loudly that people stared, she gathered up towels, rug, cool bag and Jon's clothes. Arms full, she snapped at Tilly to follow. More people were looking now and a woman shouted something but she ignored her. With Tilly tugging at the hem of her skirt, each step was an effort and her sandals sunk into the hot sand. They made their way to the life-guard station where two bronzed young men in shorts and bright yellow vests chewed gum and looked bored as she babbled her story. Yet because she was worried that any minute Jon would just appear and she'd look stupid, in a perverse way their indifference was reassuring. By now Tilly was snivelling so Jess went to the kiosk and bought her a giant red lolly shaped like a baby's dummy which she'd been nattering for ever since they'd arrived. She got red all round her mouth and chin which made her skin look as though it was raw and inflamed.

They waited. Jess was asked to repeat her story. Calls were made, other authorities consulted and by five o'clock the two lifeguards started to look worried. The police arrived. More calls. Eventually she was told the coastguard was calling in a search helicopter. Although they tried to persuade her to return to the flat, Jess insisted on staying. She bought Tilly a stick of rock and a Coke, both things of which Jon strongly disapproved, but rotten teeth seemed the least of her worries. As the beach emptied and the sun was swallowed by the hori-zon, the front started to become busier with those out for the night: skinny girls with bare midriffs and roses tattooed on their ankles tottered along arm in arm with strutting young men, all gelled hair and swelling biceps; neon lights flashed; cars crawled along the front with windows down, booming drum and bass and along the front strings of white fairy lights, looped between lampposts, quivered from the noise. Tilly leant against Jess, thumb in mouth, mesmerised. A rowdy group of girls passed and the one with the pink sash and angel wings bent over and raised her skirt to reveal bare buttocks. Jon would have been disgusted but Jess envied them their lack of shame and a perverse kind of innocence.

'What if he comes back and finds we're gone?' she kept repeating to the nice policewoman assigned to them and she didn't need to see the pity in the other woman's eyes to realise how foolish her words sounded. Eventually a police car took them back to the flat. Tilly had to be carried up the stairs, something Jon had done just the night before. She was heavy, loose-limbed, and Jess buried her face in the child's neck, inhaling the sweet yeasty smell. They slept together that night and Jess would always remember the grittiness of the sand on Tilly's feet rubbing up against hers.

The moment she saw the policewoman coming up the steps early the next morning Jess knew. A small knot of people were below on the pavement, one man with a camera might have been a reporter. She contemplated lowering the window, sticking her head out and telling them all to get lost but she didn't. The policewoman was so kind and sometimes Jess thought of going back to Cornwall to try and find out her name: it was seventeen years ago but there had to be records. She couldn't help wondering how many other bodies she'd seen in the intervening years. She was young so he might have been her first.

He was washed up on the early morning tide and an autopsy two days later revealed that he'd drowned, most probably from a heart attack. Before, if someone had said 'heart attack' she'd have pictured a fat middle aged man with a spongy red nose who smoked and drank too much, not a thirty-five year old who jogged and only drank green tea. As for 'drowned' that meant rough seas, towering waves and strong currents, not water flat as skin.

Her clearest memories from that time were random: the buckle on her sandal broke which made her sob until her cheekbones ached; the hotel did wonderful poached eggs on toast for breakfast. She and Tilly both became addicted to playing that arcade game where you shove a coin through a slot to try and dislodge a massive heap of other coins that are teetering on the edge and look as though just a breath will make them all cascade into the tray. The fact that they never succeeded was somehow reassuring. Tilly was offered a trip around the bay on the pirate ship and was really excited but at the last moment refused to go, fat tears squeezing out from under her eyepatch. Jess was upset and let her know, something she recalled with shame.

Within a week the police enquiries were completed and arrangements were made to bring Jon's body home. When they came to check out, the hotel manager said there was no charge and Jess yearned to embrace him even though he was a wizened little man with stale breath and dandruff flecked on his shoulders. In the car on the way back, the passenger seat was empty as Tilly had insisted on her usual place in the back. It was strange having that space at her side, like there was a bit of the jigsaw missing, not one that stopped you seeing the whole picture but the one needed to make it complete. A bit of sky perhaps. Once on the M3 she automatically reached out her hand to squeeze Jon's knee, just one of their silly little rituals that indicated an understanding that they were on their way home and that everything was OK.

Ahead was a bridge and as they drew near she could see that someone had sprayed *Fuck Off* in yellow paint on the metal and it was this that Jess suddenly found unbearably tragic: that someone had risked their life to hang over the side of the bridge and write that message of hate. She knew that she and Jon's story was not one of high romance. He didn't so much propose to her as suggest that the two of them would make a good team. Yet she had been desperate to escape from her parents and from her job at Waitrose and in fact he was right: they'd had a good partnership. Admittedly both of them found it difficult to use the word 'love', but anyway what was love except four letters, in that sense no different to those painted on the bridge. It was then that she could have cried properly but she needed to drive her and Tilly back to the greyness of home, far away from that terrible blue sky.

Judge's comments:
Patchy. Some good writing in places but nothing special. Some awkwardness of expression.
Shortlist   Yes / No

---

* * *

I'd like to have said the sky was 'azure' or 'Wedgwood' blue but those are clichés and what I have now learnt is that you should always avoid clichés in your writing and go for something original. (But death is hardly original: there were 420 water related deaths that year and 31 of those were people swimming.)

So instead the sky became the title of my story, parts of which are true and parts of which are not. It matters little. Surely it is only what we all do every day: strive to construct a version of reality that depicts how we would like others to see us? Writers are no different, frantically stitching one piece of life to another, discarding those that don't make any sense and that they don't want to remember and imagining new ones with brighter colours and richer textures.

Honeypot

THE BRILLIANT IDEA of stringing Jim up in the Folk Museum came later. Obviously my first job was to kill him and God knows just deciding how to do that occupied my mind for several weeks. But I'd read and watched enough crime stuff to know that the key to success was not rushing things.

Naturally when I first found out I wanted to take the bread knife and slit his throat with the serrated edge, preferably while the great useless lump was dozing in front of the telly. I fantasised about clubbing him over the head with the bread board while his back was turned and hearing the satisfying crack when the hard wood met his soft skull; or grabbing him by the scruff of the neck and forcing his stupid face onto a hotplate, holding him there and watching his skin bubble and blister. However, I sensibly bided my time turning out more bread cakes, donuts and loaves than The Yorkshire Pantry could ever hope to sell, even if it had been high season. I pounded that dough like you wouldn't believe, pulled it, stretched it and slapped it onto the work surface from a height imagining it was his scrotum. The Sunday after I'd made the discovery and when I'd been hard at it since early morning, Jim came in and said he'd have his dinner in the front room. The kitchen was that hot it felt like we were actually inside one of the ovens.

'Suit yerself,' I said, punching the air out of a newly proved loaf, 'It's only tuna salad anyroad.'

Jim gave one of his deep sighs and ambled towards the

hallway but not before he'd asked if I'd like the window opening.

'If I wanted it opening, I'd have done it meself,' I snapped.

Jim looked at me and made as if he was going to say something but then obviously decided not to. I was suddenly aware that my face was probably beetroot and I most likely had flour in my hair and all over my face. Jim used to stroke my cheek and say I had the softest skin in The Dales. Mind, that was after three pints of Theakstons. A long time ago and a lot of water under the bridge since then. Now he sighed again, a timely reminder that I'd be giving myself away if I wasn't careful.

'I can do you a jacket spud if you like. When I've done this next batch.'

His face brightened, 'That would be grand, love. If it's not too much trouble.'

Huh! He's a fine one to talk about trouble after what he did.

It's hard thinking about killing someone you've known since you were bairns. Jim and I were both Ridston born and bred. I wouldn't call us childhood sweethearts because for a long time we were more like brother and sister but we both went to the local primary, then the same High School in Richmond. Not the grammar though unlike His Lordship I did pass the 11+ and could have tried for a place. I don't remember why I didn't but girls like me were expected to leave school at fifteen and get a job locally before getting wed so that's what I did, first of all working on the till in a fruit and veg shop in Richmond, then coming back to the village to serve at The Pantry, eventually buying it from old Mrs Lowther after she had a nasty fall and had to retire. Jim and me didn't start what you might call properly courting until he went off to Tech College to do his joinery course and then we were engaged for nearly three years. Eventually I had to give him an ultimatum – name the date or sod off. His Mum, nasty cow, urged him to take the sodding off option but for once he stuck to his guns. The following June we were married at Ridston Parish Church with a reception at the Village Hall. I baked me own wedding cake and some say it were the best they ever tasted. Jim and I had our moments but we were never what you might call a romantic couple. After a couple of years of marriage it was me who always had to make the first move – if you know what I mean.

Mam still lives in the cottage where me and my two brothers were brought up, just the other side of the beck while Jim's folks, a bit posher than my family, lived in *The Gables*, a handsome double fronted house of Yorkshire stone. Jim's Dad passed away a couple of years back and his Mum struggled to keep the place on but eventually had to admit defeat. Anyhow, even before that she'd started going funny, some nights wandering round the village in her nightie or shouting at visitors from the upstairs window and chucking pillows at them. Turned out she had Alzheimer's or dementia, one of those. Jim had to put her in a home but she only lasted six months. Got a really nasty tummy bug. Mind, as I said to Jim after the funeral, it was a blessing in some ways. He didn't like that and that was one of the few times we had a real set to. Said he was 'traumatised' by his mother's death which was pathetic seeing what an old bat she was.

We could have moved into *The Gables*: that's what a lot of folk expected but I had plans and those plans did not include spending the rest of my days being a skivvy in a big house. If there were grandkids, fair enough, but me and Jim would have rattled around somewhere that size. Property prices had gone ridiculous in the last few years and with money from the sale we could make ourselves a small fortune. For a start off, I had in mind one of those cruises to the Greek islands. I could just picture meself on the sundeck, a cocktail in one hand, a saucy novel in the other. Then a new car: nothing too flashy, just a smart little runabout. Then one of them gastric band thingies followed by a new lot of clothes. It kept me awake at night wondering whether perhaps it would be better to have the op before the cruise.

But my big ambition, the one that made my pulse race, was to give The Yorkshire Pantry a complete overhaul. It hadn't been doing well for some time now and it was no good Jim saying that it was down to the recession when I knew it needed everything replacing from the dirty old lino on the floor to the old-fashioned glass display cabinets. But it would take money and that was not something we'd had much of during our married life. Jim took a bit of persuading but eventually the *For Sale* board went up outside *The Gables*. As soon as it did, I got started on my plans for The Pantry, ringing sign makers and shop fitters and getting quotations. I dreamt of it being the finest bakery in the area.

Looking back I see now that Jim had already started a campaign to rob me of The Pantry, winding me up by saying I didn't need to work anymore. I told him he could sit on his fat backside all day watching daytime telly, but I wasn't ready to hang up my apron yet. The bakery is the only thing in my life I'm proud of. Six days of the week I fill it with lovely bread, made in the same way that bread has always been made: with simple ingredients and shaped with hands that love it. But of course he never understood all that. How could he? If he had, he would never have done what he did.

Ridston is what you might call a honeypot. Meaning that it attracts a lot of visitors who park their cars in a cluster on the green and, having gazed at the view for a few minutes, then swarm over the village oohing and aahing as they poke their noses into, and I quote, *'this typical Dales village with stunning views.'* In fact we have two teashops, an ice-cream parlour, three gift shops (one consisting completely of imported tat), a pottery and the Tourist Information Centre which boasts an exhibition of local artistic talent – or rather lack of it. And the Folk Museum. The only good thing to say about the visitors is that they do spend their brass. Then there's the walkers and cyclists, poncing about in their coloured cagoules and stupid woolly hats, feeling smug that they've not taken the easy option, even though a lot of them will spend their day-to-day lives polluting the towns and cities with their 4x4s. That lot don't spend as much, with the worst ones bringing their own food and sitting on the green unwrapping a foil packet of sandwiches and drinking tea from a flask. Bastards.

When we were courting me and Jim used to visit the Folk Museum. It was out of season, which meant there'd hardly be any visitors with it being so hard to find, tucked away down a lane behind one of the tearooms. There used to be a handbell outside on the doorstep which you were meant to ring to say you're there, but we'd ignore that and just go in. In our day the place was even more of a mess and it was easy to snuggle down in a corner. 'Course Jim was always trying to get into me knickers – I'd have been disappointed if he hadn't done – but by the same token he'd have been surprised if I'd let him. That's how it was in them days.

'Museum' is a grand word for what amounts to just three small rooms. Over the years people have donated bits and pieces and Maggie, who runs it with the help of volunteers, has done her best but basically it's a clutter of random junk: rusty old milking equipment, lumps of rock, maps, old photos of the village, crockery, teapots, piles of Yorkshire Tourist Board leaflets. Most of the rubbish is labelled in glass cases or on display boards but there's some stuff that nobody knows what it is. Daft, trying to recreate for visitors what people think life was like in the village.

Once I'd killed Jim getting the body there was going to be tricky but I planned on using a wheelbarrow – at night, of course. I've never been what you might call a small woman, even when I was a young lass, and now I'm what Mam calls 'well covered'. All my baking has given me strong arms and beneath the bracelets of fat around my wrists are tendons that are as strong and elastic as dough. I'd got a key for the place – another clever move on my part. I'd heard that Maggie was going on holiday and so offered to keep an eye on things. Maggie was ever so grateful.

I wanted everyone to see him there. Three weeks ago, *The Darlington and Stockton Times* had run a front page article about how Yorkshire Cultural Heritage was considering a grant for The Museum which would provide interactive portals (whatever they might be) a gift shop, a café, toilets and a proper reception desk – all those things which organisations like that consider essential for a visitor attraction. Local people had been invited along to look at plans and offer their views on the proposed development. So what better visitor attraction could there be than Jim, mounted on the wall, as an example to all husbands who consider double crossing their wives?

Jim's betrayal was simple and brutal: he agreed to sell *The Gables* to someone who he knew was going to turn it into a bakery. Of course I didn't know anything about that until the deal was agreed and on finding out I thought I would explode with rage.

'But she's giving us a great price! 'Jim protested when at last I'd recovered enough to take him to task.

'So? Money's not everything! It's not too late to back out, Jim, please!'

'I don't want to back out.'

It was the only time I'd begged him for something and the only time he was as stubborn as a bloody mule. There was no shifting him. Later I could never work out whether this had all been a cunning plan on Jim's part to put The Pantry out of business or whether the physical assets of Sylvia Mannington, the buyer, had blinded his judgement. A divorcee in her thirties, she was blonde, by choice, and had breasts which continually looked like they were trying to escape from the snug fitting and low cut tops she always wore. Her bum was better contained but seemed to move independently from the rest of her body. I'm not surprised Jim fell for her smooth London talk. In all probability he didn't think the whole thing through. Sometimes Jim could be as thick as clotted cream.

When Sylvia visited at weekends I made a point of befriending her so that I could find out about her strategy. She was only too willing to tell me. Apparently her bakery would only use the very finest of organic flour to make loaves with names like gruyere and red onion produced in a collective near Manchester and delivered fresh every morning; she would also stock speciality chutneys, olives and oils and have baskets of free range eggs and fresh herbs on the counter. She explained in detail to me how she planned to give it a rustic feel with scrubbed boards and details of special offers written on blackboards. She wasn't my type, of course, and she was never going to be anyone other than what we call round here an offcumden or incomer and I wondered what would happen if she had an accident. Those high heels she tottered around in could be deadly! But at the end of the day it wasn't Sylvia I had a quarrel with. She was even nice enough to say that she hoped we wouldn't be in competition with one another. No, I agreed, there certainly wasn't any competition. A posh bakery would go down a bomb.

Once I'd got Jim's body into the museum and mounted it I planned to label it as 'Traitor.' Black letters on white card. And I intended to stuff a bread roll in his mouth. Not nice, I know, but I've never claimed to be nice. I used to wonder if having children would have made me nice – it does to some women. But as the years went by I stopped wondering and just got on with making my bread. It's funny but whenever I get a chance to cuddle a baby I press my nose into its neck and inhale because a baby's neck smells warm and yeasty, just like bread fresh from the oven.

It never happened, of course, the killing and Jim becoming a museum exhibit. I should have known he would find a way of thwarting my plans just like he always did. He had a fatal heart attack in the solicitor's office, just after having signed the contract of sale on *The Gables* so denying me the chance to tell him how I really felt. Or to explain about his mother, how the freshly baked breadcake filled with ham and mushroom that I brought in for her the week before she died was never intended to do her any good. I'm a country girl which means that I know all about which mushrooms to pick and which to avoid.

So, I've got the money and the world's my oyster as they say but I haven't done anything yet. I closed The Pantry on the day of Jim's funeral and don't see any point in re-opening. The R and the Y have fallen off the sign and some teenage yobs have chalked an S in the gap. Village life goes on, Sylvia's doing good business and the Museum is closing very shortly for its revamp.

Sometimes I think I might do some baking. I get out my flour bins, scoop some cupfuls into a bowl, make up some yeast and start mixing but it never seems to hold together very well.

Scarborough Warning

IT'S GROSS, THE way he eats his Mr Whippy. First off, he studies it like it's a Maths problem. As soon as it starts to melt he sticks out his tongue and does a massive circular lick. Again and again he licks until there isn't a peak anymore. Then he darts his tongue in and out like a lizard and gently pushes the ice cream down into the cone. When he's nearly finished, he turns the last bit of cone upside down and sucks out the last bit of ice cream. Suppose it's like what he does to me so you'd think it'd be sexy. It's so not.

There's other things that piss me off – like the way he folds his clothes up neatly when he's undressing or how he counts out coins when he's paying for something or when he loses his rag if someone pinches his parking space. Just chill out I want to say.

But I mean obviously he's going to have a different outlook on life and I guess that's what attracted me in the first place. And anyway there's loads of things about him that are cool like the way he took charge when we booked in at the guest house and the cow behind the reception desk gave us a dirty look; or the day we went out in the boat because I said I couldn't stick being inside all the time and the guy in charge, the captain or what-ever, said we couldn't sit near the front even though there were seats free. So J insists, politely mind, that if we can't sit where we want to then we'll have our money back. Course, we actually did get to be at the front even if it meant we were soaked from the spray. Not that it mattered – we had such a great laugh. You see, you wouldn't get Year 11 lads having the bottle to front up to someone in charge: they go around acting the big man but at the end of the day it's all just talk.

Scarborough's dead good. I didn't even know where it was until J showed me on Google Maps. In some ways it's just like any other seaside place with amusements, the fair, donkey rides and that. And seasides can be tacky. Mum and Dad used to take me and Jen to Southsea which was fine when we were kids but when we got old enough we realised how naff it was. Scarborough has a big sweep of a bay and up on the hill there's a castle looking down, frowning like a Headteacher watching all the kids at breaktime. I said that to J but I wish I hadn't.

And there's some posh bits with cobbled streets – J took us for a walk into the Old Town and that was really romantic, even though I broke one of my heels. So it's not like he's brought me somewhere tacky.

The gulls get on my nerves, though. Their screeching goes right through me. Starts first thing in the morning. And they're massive! Our second night we were eating chips on the front, I dropped one and before I knew it a bloody great gull swooped down and was pecking at my feet. It had a horrible dirty yellow beak and evil black eyes and I said I wanted to go and eat in a café or a pub but J said we couldn't and that's when we had our first row.

'Anyway, you're too young to be in a pub.'

'What you on about? We've met up in pubs loads of times before!' We used to drive to little quiet country ones.

'It's different now.'

'So last week it was OK for me to be in a pub and this week it isn't. That's stupid.'

'No, it's sensible. Eat the rest of your chips.' J frowned and my heart turned over but I wasn't letting him off the hook. I've always been the stubborn one. Gets me into a lot of trouble, that does.

'I'm not hungry anymore.'

'You said you were starving!'

'Well I lied then didn't I? You should know all about that!' I stood up and the rest of my chips fell to the ground.

'Keep your voice down! You're making a fool of yourself.'

'I don't give a toss!' I shouted over my shoulder as I walked away.

But of course I did. That was the problem. I crossed the road without looking properly and a car horn blared so I gave its driver the finger. Hoping and praying J would follow me, I went into one of the amusement arcades. The noise hurt my ears: coins falling, bells and buzzers ringing, the heavy clunk as the fruit machine handles were tugged down, a bingo caller, Lady Gaga's 'Bad Romance' blaring out. I stood in front of a glass case near the entrance. Inside the case was a big grabber thing suspended over a load of soft toys – rabbits, bears, teddies. You could tell they were tat: the fur trim on some of them was manky and on others the eyes hadn't been glued on straight. They all lay there on top of one another and it made me think of a picture we'd seen in History of the bodies in a concentration camp. I hadn't cried then, not like some of the lasses did, but I wanted to now. So I dug in my pocket, found a pound coin and rammed it into the slot. Some crappy tune came out and shakily the grabber started to move. There was a wheel which you used to direct it but I knew that wouldn't make any difference so I just stood there and watched as the claws descended onto the toys and closed over nothing. Then the grabber slowly creaked its way back to the top and the music abruptly stopped.

'How fucking pointless is that!' I don't know whether I said that aloud or just in my head. It was so noisy and I was so tired.

Then I felt the pressure of J's hands on my shoulders and I closed my eyes. His breath was hot as he kissed the back of my neck. I got a whiff of his aftershave, my lower belly went tight and funny and then everything was all right again. Sort of.

J likes discussing the past so he talks about Scarborough when we're having our evening walk. I'm OK with that. Thinking about the future is scary and as he says it's important to make the most of what we've got now. So he tells me that the town was founded around 966 AD by a Viking raider and that in the fourteenth century Edward II gave the castle to his gay lover. Fancy giving someone a bloody castle! That's really awesome. Then in the Middle Ages a fair started. J starts humming a song:

'Are you going to Scarborough Fair? Parsley, sage, rosemary and thyme…'

'What's that then?'

'Don't you know it?'

'Duh! No. Obviously. Or I wouldn't be asking.'

'It's very famous.'

'Not to me it isn't.'

But I didn't get mad. I like the way he knows so much about everything. Like a Scarborough warning which is when you get no notice of an attack. Apparently that happened to the castle once.

'So when you and me fell for each other it was like a Scarborough warning?'

'Sort of. Now that there is The Grand Hotel,' He's got his arm draped over my shoulders and he squeezes my right shoulder as he points upwards 'When it was built in 1867, it had four towers to represent the seasons, 12 floors for months of the year, 52 chimneys for weeks and 365 bedrooms for the days of the year.'

'You're kidding me!'

'I'm not. It's true. And it has a blue plaque outside to mark the fact that Anne Brontë died there.'

'We're doing *Wuthering Heights* for AS next year.'

'Anne Brontë didn't write *Wuthering Heights*. That was Emily.'

'I know that!' I lied. 'I was just saying. Jesus...'

'Sorry, I didn't mean to...'

'...act like such a know-all dick?'

He laughs, 'Guilty as charged.'

'Anyway,' I continue, 'That's if I do choose English. I know I want to do Music and History but...' I notice he's doing that frown again which darkens his face and makes me feel a bit anxious so I change the subject, 'I wish we could stay there!'

'Maybe next time.' He's curt. Sometimes the mood suddenly shifts between us like a dark cloud covering the sun. 'Time to head back.'

Things are changing. It's nearly the end of season and some of the cafes and arcades have been boarded up just in the week we've been here. It's getting darker earlier and as we walk back along the beach lights twinkle out at sea and the water scuds and hisses onto the sand. A few other people pass us but we keep our heads down and it's like we're just shadows passing other shadows.

It's not like I haven't considered the fact that J and I might be found out. I'm not some dumb bitch who hasn't thought it all through. There's always consequences, I know that. And for a long time, in a weird kind of way, I've wanted all the secrecy to end: the lies, the covering up, the hiding. Not even my best mates know for certain, though I think they guessed something is going on, and as for Mum and Dad just the thought of how apeshit they'll go can make me feel sick. But when it happened I wanted it to be calm, to be like when a piece of music comes to the end and there's just that final note which rests in the moment before silence.

I never imagined the police sirens and the screech of tyres mixing with the screech of gulls and two policemen running over the sand to grab J and frogmarch him up the slipway to the railings and then spreading his arms wide apart and handcuffing him to the railings. Never. And they didn't need to have done all the heavy stuff because he just stands there quietly, head bowed not giving them any trouble. Not like me. I scream and curse as a policewoman puts her arms around me and tries to persuade me to go with her to the waiting police car with its crazy blue circling lights. I refuse, she says something into her mouthpiece and within minutes another car skews to a stop and two more policemen get out and make their way down the beach. Blinking away tears, I shrug off the policewoman and walk by myself towards the road, sand pulling at my feet. Once at the car I try another tactic, letting the tears run down my face and begging to be allowed to speak to J. A small knot of people has gathered to gawp and I hate them. I fucking hate them. I never imagined how grubby and used I would feel – not by him but by them.

Later, travelling back south in the custody of a social worker with bad breath and striped towelling socks I pretend to be asleep and hear her on the phone talking about *'charges of child abduction'* and *'in loco parentis'* and although I know what those words mean I also know that there are no words that can hack it here, no words that can describe what J and I have. Later still I try and tell them that I will wait because I love him.

'You just thought you did,' they say, 'it was infatuation. It was what we call an inappropriate relationship.'

I watched a clay pigeon shoot once and that's how I picture what happened to J and me: they threw our lives up into the air, took careful aim and then shot them into little pieces. But the funny thing is I still like the seaside. We even go back to Scarborough occasionally. In the five years since that weekend very little has changed. The cliffs, sky, sea, sand: they're just the same. Loads will have happened on that beach and not just bad things like arrests, drinking, needles, hitting, punching, the guy who drowned a couple of years ago trying to rescue his dog. For most of the time there'll have been little kiddies building sandcastles and digging trenches at the water's edge, Dads playing footy with their sons, Mums minding the picnic and watching over their children. Family stuff.

J's never too keen on returning and of course I get that. But, I tell him, we don't look any different to all the other boring married couples who sit side by side on the benches, gazing out to sea as if it holds the answer to some unnamed problem. Now we can afford a decent B&B or even a hotel where we can sign ourselves in as Mr and Mrs and not worry about what people think because the gold band on my finger is for real. There's no reason not to hold our heads up high.

Whenever I talk like that J doesn't reply but takes my hand, raises it to his lips and kisses it. This is not a romantic gesture: he is contradicting me. He is saying that we are not like other couples. J was my teacher, I was underage and because of that the bastards put him on trial and then sent him to prison. And when he came out, as if he hadn't gone through enough, they put him on the Sex Offender Register. Which I think is quite ironic seeing how little sex we have these days. As a result of being on the register he can only do casual work – cash in hand, no questions asked – and I'm on the till at Morrisons. A-levels and University never happened. It would have been humiliating to stay on at school and it just showed how little everyone, especially Mum and Dad, knew me if they thought I'd give up that easily. Anyway, Jen has done the right thing. She's at Oxford now which should make up for the disappointment that is me.

I've noticed recently how J's hands have changed. Partly it's the manual work he does now. Before, when his fingers tapped on computer keys or held a pencil, they were quite soft. Now his fingerpads have hard ridges. When he touches my face the roughness snags on my skin and I have to take care not to flinch. But also the back of his hands have become a bit more translucent. If I take his hand and move it this way and that I can see the veins like thin blue snakes under the skin. Of course there are other signs that time has passed, like the creases around his eyes and mouth, but it's his hands I notice the most. When I told him this he said that mine had changed too and when I looked I saw that, as usual, he was right. When I used to play the piano every day my fingerpads were hard but now they're soft, almost pulpy.

When we hold hands and our fingers entwine, it's like we have swapped skins.

I prefer going to Scarborough in winter, watching the waves pound the sea wall on North Bay, walking as near as I can and then jumping away if an especially large breaker rears over the wall and crashes down onto the walkway. I know I make J scared by doing that so if I feel like being a real cow I do it a lot and wait to see how long he can go without pulling me back onto the safety of the road. Once we visited in February and on the Saturday afternoon J said he wanted to visit the Rotunda Museum. I wasn't keen but sometimes it's just easier to give way. At any rate, there wasn't anything else to do and it was freezing. So we paid our money and went in. Turned out it's full of geological specimens and I thought – Oh God, boring or what – so I wandered off and just drifted around playing on my phone which is guaranteed to drive J mad. Every so often I came across him, working his way round the exhibitions, putting his glasses on and then taking them off as he alternately peered at the labels and then stood back to look at the bits of rock. Before, he would have told me all about them but not anymore. There was hardly anyone else there so it was lovely and peaceful and gradually I stopped wandering and sat down, finding to my surprise how much I liked the place: the curvature of the walls, the lack of corners. It felt like being cocooned in a time capsule. I kept thinking of all the great lumps of stone that had been hacked out from the cliffs or dug up from quarries which would have been covered in mud, moss, bugs and all kinds of shit; how they would have had to be cleaned and polished before being put in the glass cases so that they could be admired. There were hidden lights – blue, amber and violet – that showed the specimens off to their best, that made them gleam as if they came from different planets and had magical powers.

In the end I actually wanted to stay longer but the guy on the door came up and said it closed early in winter. He turned off the lights behind us and I gave a quick glance back. No magic. Everything looked dull and ordinary: just a collection of grey rocks sitting under dusty glass. When we came out J lingered in the doorway asking the guy how long the Rotunda had been there and so on. While we'd been inside it had started snowing – the ground was already freckled with a thin covering. I looked at the sea which was framed by one of the arches of Valley Bridge. That's the bridge a lot of people used to jump from before they put up a high fence either side but some saddos still manage to get over. People will always find a way if they are desperate enough.

'Do you regret it?' J sometimes asks when he's feeling particularly low.

'Of course not,' I reply. What else can I say?

View from the Top

With a judder the Big Wheel stops, our gondola at the top. It rocks gently and creaks, wood against wood. My hands clutch the bar that gates us and my knuckles whiten.

'Hold my hand,' he says jokingly, trying to prise my fingers off the bar.

I resist and the carriage sways with our movements. The red paint of the bar is blistered and sharp-edged flakes are embedded in the soft fleshiness of my thumb pads.

'What a view! You can see for miles!'

Now he's trying to divert me, like you would a child, so for a few moments I act the child, refusing to look where he's pointing. Then, grudgingly, I do. The fair is at the far end of the front, on a piece of land that juts out and curves inwards slightly, like a lobster claw. On two sides the sea surrounds us, flat and blue. Fishing boats, windsurfers and a pirate pleasure boat criss-cross the bay, trailing frills of foam. At low tide the crescent of beach is littered with holiday makers: deck chairs, towels, air beds and windbreaks mark out postage stamps of territory; small children dabble and dig at the water's edge, scampering away in mock terror when the surf breaks, overseen by adults who stand with arms folded indulgently. I focus on a young couple as they run into the water holding hands, kicking up spray; she breaks free and plunges under and he follows. Then they swim outwards, side by side, their arms cleaving the water.

'And look down there!'

Below us the other fair rides are like mechanical toys spread out on a carpet. The Waltzer raises and dips its multiple arms causing the orange and purple cars to spin while swing boats inscribe semicircles, cups and saucers slowly rotate and on the carousel the horses slide sedately up and down their twisted barley-sugar poles. Periodically one of these toys will stop, disgorge people into the clump who have been waiting, siphon off others and then, rewound, will start up again.

'I feel a bit sick,' I say. I don't but it's a sure-fire way of getting him to stop fooling around.

'Do you? Just lean back and take some deep breaths. You'll be fine.'

I do as he says and close my eyes. Tinny music carries upwards along with muffled traffic and crowd noise, as insubstantial as the candy floss we shared earlier. I've always loved the sluttiness of the amusements so before the fair we worked our way along the various arcades and Bingo halls on the seafront, all of them touting for business and each one louder and flashier than the last. We played on fruit machines, though I had such little strength that he had to stand behind me and help pull the levers down; we sent coin after coin skittering down to land on top of others which must surely this time topple over; he tried and failed to win a prize for me by manoeuvring a claw onto a pile of cheap stuffed toys; we bought baseball hats and giant lollipops for the kids and later had chips for our dinner, sitting on the sea wall, swinging our legs and carrying on like a couple of honeymooners.

I'd wanted to come here. When my treatments were at their worst, he asked me where I'd like to go.

'Anywhere,' he said, 'I'll take you anywhere. Just name

the place. Somewhere hot? Exotic? How about the Car-
ibbean?'

But I needed to come to this seaside town where
I'd spent so many childhood holidays and where we'd
brought our own kids on day trips. In my imagination, I
could see Mum and Dad and the kids down there on the
beach amongst all those other specks of humanity.

'It might be the last time,' I said.

'Don't you dare talk like that!' he raged, 'You're being
melodramatic as usual. I won't have it!'

'I'm only being realistic, love.'

I open my eyes and it's like coming round from the
anaesthetic when you re-emerge into a world that is familiar and yet at the same time new, freshly painted. A
sudden gust of wind rocks the gondola and this time I
can sense that he is worried too.

He cloaks his anxiety with bluster, 'This is ridiculous!
We've been stopped for bloody ages. If there's something
wrong we should have been told!'

His neck reddens when he's angry and a small muscle
twitches in his cheek. He's been angry at the doctors,
the consultant, even the angels who look after me in the
Daycare Unit. He's had enough anger for all of us and,
although there were times when I've been upset and embarrassed, I also love him even more for it.

'It'll be OK,' I say and I moisten the tip of my finger
with my spit and gently rub at the crinkle at the side of
his eye where some flecks of dried salt have lodged.

The Wheel gives a fierce jolt. For a second or two we
remain at the top of the world, above us just sky and
more sky, and then we crest the moment and slowly begin to descend. It is painfully slow and jerky and about
a third of the way down again we stop. We are in limbo,

caught between the past and future, between knowing and not knowing, and suddenly it is unbearable. Without the need to say anything, the two of us lean our bodies forward against the bar and then lean back. Forward and back, forward and back. We are in perfect unison. Our gondola is building up momentum with its rocking, almost as if it is no longer joined to the others, and I am vaguely aware of some shouting and screaming from down on the ground. Then the ride re-starts properly and gathers speed, perhaps too much speed, and we are hurtling downwards. The ground is rushing up to meet us and I'm aware of a blur of colour and noise, our hands laced together, the rubbing of our wedding rings.

A Blue Dress

I LOVE WHAT I do. I take trouble. Spit on my boots. Rub my underarms with a rag. Flatten my hair. Not everyone takes pride like me. But I'm being looked at. In that courtroom, all eyes are directed towards the place where I stand and for the first time in my life it is me who's centre stage. When I fetch one of the women and we start the walk up the steps into the dock, me holding her arm just firmly enough to steady but not enough to hurt, the gentle hum of the crowd is like a swarm of bees. I make sure I don't hurry the moment and make my footsteps as heavy and deliberate as possible. As everyone becomes aware of our approach, the hum ceases and all you can hear is the creak of the benches as people crane to see and outside the screaming of kittiwakes as they swoop underneath Tyne Bridge. The whole place holds its breath. Then we step up into the light and are greeted by a roar. People stand and stamp their feet. They point and there's hissing. Shouting. Chanting.

'Witch! Witch! Witch!'

That's often the moment when one of the weakest will swoon and it's up to me to catch her before she hits the deck. I have a vial of something the apothecary gave me which I hold under her nose and that usually brings her round quick enough. Then I have to prop her against the railing. Usually she's as light as a feather so it's not hard to do. For others the crowd reaction seems to give them strength: they grip the rail and face out their accusers, sometimes even trading insults with them. Their fate is decided even before the proceedings begin.

People want to know what it's like touching the women. Do any of them fight you, they ask. What if you get spit on you? It might be deadly venom! Are they shaking? Screaming? Do they ever mess themselves? Aren't you afraid of being magicked? What if they put a curse on you and your family?

What I do is to keep the nosy parkers waiting as long as I can but you have to be careful. Leave it too long and they'll go looking for someone else who was there – or claims they were. Everyone's looking to make something out of this business. Of course, I get them to buy me ale before I really start to talk. It's thirsty work, I'll say, and I pinch at my throat like it hasn't had a drop down it for days. I shouldn't be saying anything, I tell them. After all, it's idle talk that caused some of the accused to be where they are today. Only some, mind. At this point I pause to make it more dramatic and that's always when my listeners lean forward, eyes popping out of their skulls, greedy as a pack of jackals to hear the grisly details. Others are messing with the Devil for sure, I say. How do you know, they ask, and that's when I put my fingers, oh so slowly, to my lips.

'I can tell,' I say, lowering my voice almost to a whisper and I close my eyes.

When I open them again, my audience has melted away, afraid. But there will always be others, eager to hear my tales. Admittedly I've been spending more time than I should do in the taverns and it's in vain that I tell my wife that it's not costing us anything.

The one who ends it all for me is different. Most of those I handle are filthy crones, the type you wouldn't give a glance at if they were lying in the gutter. Witches or not, the old ones are better off dead, that's the way I like to look at it. As for the young 'uns, by the time I see them they're half way to the grave anyway: they've been pricked by the witch-finder so much that their skin is red raw and often they're bleeding, although usually they've already confessed so the pricking is neither here nor there. But this one you can't say she whether she is young or old and although she must have been pricked there's no sign of anything. She looks tired and thin, the same as all of them, but there's a stillness about her.

'My name is Mary,' she says to me when I go to fetch her from the holding cell, even though I never ask their names. She's the last one that day so is alone and she sits there, calm as you like, her manacled hands resting on her lap and her head held high for all the world as if she is in some grand dining room. She has the clearest eyes I've ever seen in my life, grey like rinsed pebbles, and when she looks straight at me it's a shock – as if she can see through me to my soul. She is wearing a simple blue shift and she smells faintly of lavender and when I think back and try to picture her in more detail – the shape of her face, the colour of her hair or how tall she was – I can't. All I remember is a blue dress and lavender.

When we appear in the courtroom the crowd response is muted. There's never the same excitement at the end of the day and some have already left. Daylight is fading but someone must have decided it wasn't worth lighting any candles. The Mayor looks bored and bad tempered. The clerk reads out the charges: that Mary White did curse her neighbour who then miscarried a child, that Mary White was seen one night by another neighbour in the guise of a wolf who ate three of her chickens, that Mary White fornicated with the devil.

Her response to the accusations and then to the witness accounts that follow is one of mild interest, as if she is listening to things said about another person but not someone with whom she has any connection. At one point she smiles a sweet smile which riles the Mayor so that he bangs the high table and says he is not prepared to hear any more testimony. When the inevitable guilty verdict comes, followed by jeers and catcalls, she just inclines her head gently as if to acknowledge a courtesy. Then she turns to me and says, 'What happens now?'

I just stare at her, open-mouthed. Surely she knows the consequences of the verdict? I don't reply as I take her back down to the cell and, once there, she repeats the question. I should lock her up and leave but the bunch of keys in my hand is so heavy that I feel weighted, like a boat chained and anchored.

'You know what is done to witches!' My voice comes out scornful and I know I sound harsh but she's acting as though she's simple when it's obvious she isn't.

'But I'm not a witch. Whatever that word might mean.' She's not upset, just stating a fact like she's saying that when the sun is highest in the sky that means it's noon.

'You've been found guilty!'

'But that's not the same as being guilty is it? What happens next?'

That confuses me and I get angry. 'Alright, I'll tell you! You'll be kept here overnight. You can see a priest if you want to. Then at sunrise tomorrow you'll be taken to Town Moor in an open cart along with four others. There each one of you will be tied to a stake. You'll be asked if you want to repent and beg forgiveness. A bonfire will be lit underneath. Then you'll … burn.' My mouth feels hot as I say that last word, as if it has been stuffed with pepper.

'I forgive you.'

The three words float in the air between us like dust motes. Keeping her eyes on me, she raises her hands, as if intending to make some kind of gesture and her manacles clink. She looks down at them in surprise, like she's forgotten they are there.

'Forgive me? I haven't done anything wrong! I'm just doing my job. Someone has to! And I carry out my duties a lot more respectfully than some. It's not me who pronounced you guilty, anyway, it was the Mayor. If I didn't do it, someone else would. You have to make a living how you can these days. I've got a family to support – how would it help them if the money stopped coming in? Anyway, I only do as I'm told.'

I am babbling and I find myself suddenly no longer angry but sad. There is even moisture in my eyes, the first time this has happened since our beloved Gretchen died of the fever at eight months. Mary sees this but she doesn't say anything. Just rests those steady grey eyes on me.

Usually I go and watch the burnings but I don't this time. The really strange thing is that when I ask my mate Ralph how it went for the five women he replies that it was a good turn out and that all of the women repented and renounced the devil even before the fires were lit. But, he adds, I'd got it wrong, there were only four women, not five. I open my mouth to argue with him but then change my mind. For some reason, I don't want to think about Mary. About who she was or what she did or didn't do. I don't want to imagine her blue dress becoming dirty or singed.

I fail to show up at the next trial the following week but every morning there's a line of people snaking round the building wanting the work. It's not so much the money, you see, but more to do with wanting to be at the heart of things, feeling that what you are doing is important and makes a difference. Within a few days I get myself fixed up unloading barges further down the river. It's hard work, starting at sun up and toiling until dark and for little reward though sometimes you get given a few potatoes or some lumps of coal when bags have split. The man in charge has a vicious temper if anyone steps out of line. But in a strange way I'm content enough.

I'm not stupid. I knew the trials were going to come to an end before too long anyway. It was all getting out of hand and I'd seen the signs: villagers not trusting each other; old grudges used as excuses; often simple blood lust. In fact, it was probably the best thing to do: leaving before the tide turned and those who were pointing the finger end up having the finger pointed at them. I do still have the occasional nightmare when flames lick at my feet and ash clags my mouth. Then I jolt awake and lie there, drenched in sweat with my skin burning and my heart racing. My wife sleeps on beside me. She is no longer a beauty, having aged as women do when they live a life as hard as ours. But she has been a better wife than I have been a husband. When I ask her how she feels about me not working in the courtroom, because I know she's boasted to people about it, she says that as long as I bring back enough to feed and clothe the children it is of no matter. Work is work, she says.

One day, when my fortune is made, I will buy her the most beautiful blue dress.

Robert Plant was at my
ex-husband's wake

In memory of Paul (1/11/1951 – 2/11/2014) who is not Eric.

IT WAS GOOD that he came, especially as not many did. I'd booked the small function room at The Royal but even that was nowhere near half full. People stood in awkward clumps, ignoring the chairs placed around the outside of the room and occasionally breaking ranks to sample the anaemic buffet laid out on a long table draped with a white cloth, an unfortunate reminder of the altar we'd all recently faced during the dreary but thankfully short funeral service. With the notable exception of Eric's neighbour Mrs Blogdon, who was taking full advantage of the free bar, most sipped tea and coffee. The hotel had provided a ghetto blaster and I'd chosen a compilation of rock anthems which should have been blaring out but the space swallowed the noise and the sound was weak and tinny competing with the clink of teaspoons and crockery. Under harsh fluorescent lights, a few self-consciously tapped their feet or nodded their heads.

Robert Plant stood tall in the doorway. Even if the walls of Eric's bungalow hadn't been covered with pictures of Plant along with his other heroes – Page, Hendrix, Morrison, Prince – I'd have known him anywhere. Ramrod straight with arms folded and his long legs encased in dusty pink denims, he looked like a gunslinger new in town and checking out the saloon bar. Against the light his hair was a tumble of grey and gold curls falling onto the shoulders of his biker jacket. For a brief moment the subdued hum of conversation ceased as everyone turned to look at the new arrival and all that could be heard was 'Born to be Wild'. Then politeness demanded that attention was re-focussed on the mushroom vol-au-vents and talk of the weather. I took a deep breath and crossed the room to Plant, unable to resist the absurd thought that it was a shame Eric wasn't here to enjoy this.

Eric had always wanted to be a rock god. His Mum told me that at nursery school he'd refused point blank to play a Wise Man, insisting that he could be Mick Jagger bringing frankincense to Baby Jesus. By the age of ten his hair stood out from his head like an electrified dandelion and he wore leather (well, plastic) trousers and shades. While on a field trip in Year 10 he had to be sent home because of throwing a TV set out of the common room window in homage to Keith Moon.

By the time I reached the great man, he had taken a few steps into the room and was frowning. On either side hovered two young PR people, a man with aviator specs and a quiff and a woman jabbing at the screen of her iPad with a red talon. Deciding that the best approach was not to make a fuss but to greet Plant just the same way I had everyone else, I proffered my hand, 'Hello there, very kind of you to come and pay your respects. Can I offer you some refreshments?'

The frown now became a deeply etched furrow. Noting this, Plant's acolytes turned into overwound mechanical toys, pacing in circles with phones clamped to their ears.

'What the fuck...?!' Quiff screeched.

'You – are – fuck – ing – kid – ding – me!' Talon said, enunciating each word loudly and clearly as if to someone lip reading.

'So this is…?' Plant's voice was softer than I'd expected with just a very faint mid-Atlantic twang.

'It was my husband's, well ex-husband's, funeral today. This is the celebration.'

I followed Plant's gaze which took in the irony of the term I'd used to describe the wake and for the first time since Mrs B's call the week before tears sprang into my eyes. Was this really all Eric's life amounted to? One old school friend who had travelled from Chester with his wife, some fellow retired librarians, a distant cousin and a few others I didn't recognise – probably from the Local History Group if their resemblance to ancient artefacts was anything to go by.

While I was having a moment and rummaging in my bag for a hanky, Phil Manners, the new Head of Librar-ies, made his way over and flapped a paper serviette in Plant's face. At the best of times, with his baby pink cheeks, Phil looked adolescent; now he acted it. Quiff and Talon closed in.

'I'm a great fan. Could I possibly get your autograph?'

'Fuck off!' This from Quiff.

'A photo with you perhaps?'

'Yeah, fuck off!' Talon.

'Cool it, dudes,' Plant said sharply then took the servi-ette and scribbled on it. 'That do you?'

'Great, thanks!'

We watched Phil's cocky walk as he rejoined his group.

'He's no fan. He'll be flogging it on eBay before the end of the afternoon,' Plant said, sounding resigned rath-er than pissed.

'How do you know? That he's not a fan, I mean.'

'You get a nose for these things.' Phil was now at the centre of a huddle of people, consulting his phone, 'He'll be checking the going rate.'

'Mr Plant, sir, we need to move you on now,' Quiff said, 'Local press call is in the main function room. Serena mistook the venue.'

'You motherfucker! I so did not!' Talon's cheeks flamed, vying to match her nail colour.

'Excuse their language,' Plant said, 'They assume they have to use profanities around me. Keep buying vodka even though I've told them Earl Grey is my drink of choice. But it looks like I need to be somewhere else. Can I just offer my condolences on your loss?'

'Thank you.'

I screwed my hanky into a ball. There was a pause but not an awkward one. Plant seemed reluctant to go.

'So tell me, what was he like, your ex-husband?'

'Eric loved rock music. More than loved. He was obsessed. He wanted to be a musician himself but ... well, he wasn't any good.'

'Not necessarily an obstacle.'

'Actually, he was bloody awful.'

It had taken me a while to become aware of this. On stage Eric was charismatic – he had the actions, the look, the attitude – while offstage he reverted to being his usual gentle and diffident self. It proved a powerful mix and I was well and truly smitten, my parents' disapproval only increasing the attraction. When Eric and I first met his heavy metal band Screaming Cabbage was well known on the local circuit but didn't seem able to make it to the next level. Only after about six months did I realise the problem: Eric. Although he played the part of a rock star faultlessly – hardly surprising after his long apprenticeship – musically he didn't have it. After the inevitable break up of Cabbage, he founded Blind Cougar then Party Animal followed by Ladlelugger and it became obvious that he couldn't join an existing band because no one would have him. After that, I lost track. Not that I even attempted to communicate any of this to my companion. Why would he care anyway? He was only being polite, excessively so in fact.

I attempted a nonchalant shrug, 'Eric spent most of his life trying to achieve something impossible. It was so frustrating…'

'But it sounds as if at least he knew what he wanted.'

'The trouble being that it wasn't the same as what I wanted. Or rather what I thought I did.'

'Ah well, I know all about problems with partners having different priorities.' He scratched his nose and sighed deeply. 'Anyhow, I'd best be moving on or the children will be throwing hissy fits.' He indicated Quiff and Talon who were slouched either side of the door, scowling.

'Of course.'

He hesitated, 'I don't suppose you'd like some tickets for tonight?'

'Tonight?'

'I'm doing a solo gig at the City Hall. Near the end of the tour, thank Christ. My back's really giving me gip.'

'I'm not sure…' I was due at the Rotary Club dinner that night with my husband and I'd already blotted my copybook big time by having wrested the funeral arrangements from Mrs B.

As I hesitated, Plant, embarrassed, mumbled, 'Sorry, probably not really appropriate today.'

I looked around the room. Mrs B was well gone, lurching from group to group retelling the tale of how she'd found Eric dead in the garden after he had tripped over a rake and hit his head on the marble statue of Ozzy. Eric's cousin and wife were consulting a timetable while others were shuffling and looking at their watches. The music had finished and other sounds drifted in from outside: laughter from the bar, the ping of lift doors opening and closing in the reception area. I thought of Eric and me; how I'd been jealous of his guitars, begrudged the money he spent on gigs and the time he spent on amassing rock memorabilia; how all that energy I'd directed against what was his life's passion seemed so pointless now, and anyway, how it was such a very long time ago. In the intervening years we'd both somehow slipped from middle age into what might shockingly be termed old age, while the rock gods on his walls, bare chested and wild haired, remained forever young.

'I think it would be highly appropriate, actually,' I said to Robert Plant, songwriter and guitarist with Led Zeppelin, whose nine albums had sold 200-300 million globally and who now boasted a face as leathery and creased as his jacket, whose hands were spattered with liver spots and who sported some grey nasal hairs badly in need of a trim.

'I'll make sure two tickets are left on the door. Nice meeting you.' He turned to go.

'Mr Plant?' I tapped him lightly on the arm, my fingers making brief contact with the roughness of his sleeve. 'Just the one ticket, please.'